Alexander Kennedy

Remarkable Convictions

SALZWASSER
VERLAG

Alexander Kennedy

Remarkable Convictions

Reprint of the original, first published in 1865.

1st Edition 2022 | ISBN: 978-3-75258-947-4

Verlag (Publisher): Salzwasser Verlag GmbH, Zeilweg 44, 60439 Frankfurt, Deutschland
Vertretungsberechtigt (Authorized to represent): E. Roepke, Zeilweg 44, 60439 Frankfurt, Deutschland
Druck (Print): Books on Demand GmbH, In de Tarpen 42, 22848 Norderstedt, Deutschland

REMARKABLE CONVICTIONS.

BY

A WRITER TO THE SIGNET.

EDINBURGH

1865.

PREFACE.

A GREAT proportion of the trials reported in the following pages, are cases which actually occurred, and were tried in criminal courts, or investigated on the part of prosecutors. Names of persons and places, however, are generally changed or suppressed, and in some of them the incidents are slightly altered. Two or three of them may be termed composite, being made up of incidents gleaned from several other known cases, and combined in one. The whole are intended to illustrate the effect of circumstantial evidence, and to shew how often facts of an apparently trivial nature, and wholly unexpected, turn up, bringing home guilt to an accused party, even in the face of an able and ingenious defence. Thus, a foot-print, the dropping of a glove, a button, a knife, a handkerchief, or the like, have frequently turned the scale of evidence against a prisoner. Nothing in the investigation of crime is more difficult to deal with, or requires the exercise of more caution, than circumstantial evidence. Indeed, in the absence of direct proof, it ought to be so abundant and full, as to preclude the possibility of any mistake or doubt. The maturest consideration of an intelligent jury, aided by the charge of an able judge, are necessary to determine the effect of testimony afforded by mere circumstances independently of direct facts. Incautious conduct in weighing proof of this description has sometimes been known to consign an innocent party to lengthened imprisonment, and even to the gibbet.

CONTENTS.

THE BLUE CLOAK.

In the year 1804, Michael Milligan, an itinerant Irish tinker, was tried before the Western Circuit Court of Justiciary (Assizes) in Scotland, charged with the murder of his wife. The Scotch forms in criminal prosecutions differ entirely from those in England, the prosecution being conducted at the expense of the Government by a Crown lawyer, termed the Lord Advocate, whose duties resemble those of the Procureur de Roi in France, and who has a number of deputes who conduct the causes when he is absent.

The indictment charged the prisoner with striking, beating, and thereafter pushing Margaret Reilly his wife, into the Crinan Canal, at or near a place called Carnbane, whereby she was drowned, or otherwise deprived of life; and that the said Michael Milligan thereby murdered his said wife. The prisoner having pleaded not guilty, a jury was impannelled.

In adducing evidence in Scotland, the prisoner is placed at a considerable disadvantage, as he does not hear what the witnesses for the crown have to say, or is confronted with them, till the trial proceeds, unless he can bear the heavy expense of obtaining a precognition, being merely furnished with a list of their names and addresses; while in England he sees them, and hears what they have to state, and may cross-examine them by himself or his law adviser previous to his committal. This defect was conspicuous in the present trial. A number of witnesses were examined who saw the murder committed from a hill on which they stood, several miles distant, and where they were engaged cutting copse-wood. They stated that they saw a man first beating, and afterwards throwing or pushing a female into the canal, and on hasteuing to the spot they found the body of the woman drowned, and identified it as that of the accused's wife, but they were too far distant to identify the prisoner as the person who committed the murder—the murderer having run off in an opposite direction the moment after the act was perpetrated. The prisoner and his wife were well known by the witnesses examined, and by all the inhabitants throughout that and the adjoining district, as itinerant pedlars who had for many years traversed the country selling horn spoons, tin jugs, and other articles of their own manufacture. This itinerating class are a numerous body in Scotland, and, like the gipsy tribes, have seldom any fixed place of abode. They generally confine themselves to two or three districts, and being known to all the farmers and other inhabitants, to whom they make themselves useful in the way of their trade, they claim and obtain lodgings from each farmer in a barn, kiln, or other outhouse. It was proved that the prisoner and his wife, who belonged to the class referred to, were in the habit of periodically visiting the district where Carnbane is situated. It appeared, however, from the cross-examination of the witnesses, that though they more generally travelled together, they not unfrequently, to save time and labour, traversed each a separate district, and that on these occasions the wife often had a male relative or friend along with her.

Another point in the case arose out of a coarse blue cloak which was worn by the man who committed the murder. The witnesses all swore that he had on such a cloak, but that when he saw them hastening to the spot, he ran to make his escape, and, in order to increase his speed, threw off the cloak, which they found on the banks of the canal. It was also proved that the accused in travelling usually wore such a cloak, but though the cloak was produced in court, none of the witnesses who saw the murder committed, could say that it was the cloak of the accused; and it so happened that, at that period, coarse blue cloaks of the same fabric and pattern were very commonly worn by almost all the lower classes in Scotland. The prisoner made no attempt to prove an *alibi*, which it was thought he might have done had he been innocent, (although the burden of proof rested with the Crown;) but this circumstance, coupled with the others, made the case amount only to one of strong suspicion. The prisoner and his counsel, therefore, thinking the proof concluded, were confident of an acquittal.

At this stage of the case, a little old man, the last name in the list of witnesses, was placed in the witness-box, on the part of the Crown. The prisoner's counsel paid little regard at first to this witness, thinking that he was merely one of those, of whom there were many already examined, who had seen the murder from a distance. On being sworn and examined, this witness said he was a tailor by trade, lived in the parish of Southend, seventy miles distant, knew the prisoner, in whose neighbourhood he resided for a number of years, and made clothes for his family. He was next asked if he had ever made a cloak for the prisoner. He said he had made a blue cloak for him about twenty years before, and that he would know it at once if he saw it. He was asked how he could identify it as the cloak made by him so long ago, seeing that such cloaks were so much alike. The case now assumed a thrilling interest, it being plain that the life of the prisoner hung upon the identification of the cloak, and the prisoner and his counsel, who had previously looked all confidence, now seemed to exhibit much anxiety. "I would," said the witness, "know that cloak among ten thousand. There was too little cloth given me to make it, and, to add to the difficulty, the cloth was in two separate pieces; and I remember I never had greater difficulty in completing any piece of dress. The consequence was, there were a great many 'eiks' or joinings in it. Several of these occurred near the buttons and button-holes, and there are two triangular pieces of cloth of a different kind, and lighter in the colour than the rest of the cloth, under the cape; the cape was also smaller than usual." The keenest anxiety was now evinced on the part of the audience to have the cloak examined. The parcel containing it was accordingly produced, and on being unfolded, the witness pointed out the two triangular joinings under the cape, of which he had spoken, the colour of which differed considerably from the rest of the cloak, and also the joinings in front, at the buttons and button-holes. He also exhibited the cape, which was much smaller than usual; and he swore that this was the identical cloak made by him for the accused twenty years before. A murmur of astonishment, mingled with abhorrence, escaped from the audience. The prisoner became lividly pale, and the confident look of his counsel was wholly abandoned. After a short address from the Advocate Depute on the part of the Crown, and from the counsel for the defence on the part of the panel; the jury, after the judge had summed up the evidence, having retired for half-an-hour, returned a unanimous verdict of wilful murder against the prisoner, who was afterwards executed at the county town of Inverary.*

* The case above noticed actually occurred in the Western Justiciary Circuit in Scotland, about the beginning of the present century. The late Lord Justice General Boyle was the Advocate Depute, who conducted the cause on the part of the Crown.

MURDER, AND CONCEALMENT OF THE BODY.

Soon after the gold discoveries in Australia, extensive immigrations of Chinese took place into that colony, and owing to their known industry and perseverance as labourers, great numbers of them obtained employment from the stockholders and other settlers. Their services were more generally in demand than would have been the case under ordinary circumstances, owing to the European servants of settlers having, in considerable numbers, deserted the service of their employers, and gone to the gold-diggings, leaving the stocks without shepherds and completely deserted, their agriculture at a stand, and their crops uncut and unsecured.

The Europeans in the employment of Mr Sime, a stockholder, on a station in the district of Bligh, on the Castlereagh river, in the colony of New South Wales, having all left him, and gone to the gold-fields, he engaged sixteen Chinamen at Sydney, to supply their places. Accordingly, with the exception of his overseer, James Bennet, a faithful and valuable servant, and two female domestics, his whole establishment of servants were Chinamen. They proved, as was expected, industrious, and, in many respects, useful; but, like most of their countrymen, greatly addicted to petty thieving, and from there being no other than Chinamen on the station, (except the overseer,) the detection and prevention of such offences became extremely difficult; accordingly, pilfering was carried on to a great extent. The overseer having at length detected several individuals in the act of thieving, two of the offenders were dismissed the service. Some of the remaining party were heard to express their strong disapprobation of the overseer's conduct, and their hatred of him; they also let slip some threats that they would take an opportunity to be avenged on account of the dismissal of their two countrymen.

In two or three days after the dismissal of the two thieves, the overseer disappeared, and could nowhere be found. A thorough search was made for him throughout the run in every place that could be thought of. Every stream, and pond, and all the woods and places of concealment were minutely examined. Inquiries were instituted at all the neighbouring stations, but to no purpose. Nobody had seen or heard of him. Advertisements were put into the Sydney newspapers, with similar results, and after the lapse of some weeks his discovery was despaired of. The Chinamen all declared they had not seen him since the time he was observed going to his house the evening before his disappearance. Though Mr Sime had the strongest suspicion that his Chinese servants had murdered his overseer, yet he could not find the slightest trace of such an act; and a favourite dog of the overseer having disappeared at the same time, led to the inference that he must have, for some unknown cause, gone off during the night, accompanied by his dog.

Whilst matters were in this position, Mr Sime was one day alone, examining some fences to be repaired in one of his large sheep-pens, in which the sheep in Australia are placed every evening for security against native dogs and thieves. His eye happening to rest on the gate-way entering into the pen, it occurred to him that the ground at the entrance was not so smooth as usual, and a little more elevated; but as the surface was walked over every morning and evening by droves of sheep, it was only after minute examination he discovered that the earth had been very recently dug or turned up. It instantly flashed on his mind that the overseer had been murdered by the Chinamen, and his body cunningly buried at the entrance to the pen, so that all traces of digging would be immediately effaced by the constant walking of a large body of sheep over the spot. Yet the disappearance of the dog, (the destruction of which by the Chinamen never occurred to him,) gave rise to many doubts and difficulties. It was, however, plain that the ground had been recently dug, without his knowledge and for some unknown purpose, and he was therefore resolved to investigate the cause.

Mr Sime found it necessary to proceed with great caution. He sent a private express to the superintendent of police of the district, to be in attendance on the second day thereafter, accompanied by a magistrate with a sufficient force, at an hour when all the Chinamen would be sent to different remote parts of the station. The superintendent and party arrived accordingly, and having dug the spot at the pen gate, there they found poor Bennet's body fearfully disfigured with wounds. They found in the same grave the carcase of his favourite dog with its master's head resting on its body. It thus appeared, that by the most thorough adroitness and cunning, the murderers had destroyed the dog, knowing that it would scent out the spot where its master's body was deposited. The police next apprehended each of the Chinamen as they could be found; and having confined each in a separate apartment, they were examined by the magistrate separately. The better conducted of them were first examined, and a complete disclosure was obtained.

It appeared that of the fourteen Chinamen then in Mr Sime's employment, ten were actively engaged in the murder. Two or three of them stabbed Bennet from behind, and the others beat him with clubs as he lay on the ground senseless, till life was completely extinct. They next stabbed and beat the dog till it was dead; and having with cunning discrimination, devised the plan of digging a hole at the entrance of the pen, where large droves of sheep were driven over every evening and morning, and all trace of their operations thus prevented, there they buried poor Bennet and his faithful dog. The whole party, with the exception of three or four who took no active part in the murder, were sent to Sydney, and brought to trial before the Supreme Court there. The two female domestics in Mr Sime's employment, proved the thefts committed by the two fellow-servants of the accused—their detection by Bennet—the strong hatred of him, and threats expressed by them in consequence thereof, and the total absence from the station of any other person on whom the slightest suspicion could rest. Mr Sime, the superintendent, and constables, proved the finding of the body at the gateway where the accused were constantly engaged. The four Chinamen who were not directly engaged in the murder, though they might be chargeable as accessories, were admitted as approvers, and gave evidence for the prosecution.

The murder being thus clearly proved, the prisoners were unanimously found guilty by the jury. Seven were hanged at Sydney, and three were sentenced to work upon the roads for ten years.*

* The murder here narrated actually occurred at the place mentioned. Seven of the prisoners were hanged as stated. The event occasioned a great sensation in the colony from the number of Chinese that were employed there at that time. Many stockholders would give them no employment after the occurrence referred to.

DETECTION OF MURDER BY NATIVE AUSTRALIANS.

THE power possessed by the native Australian in tracing fugitives or discovering anything lost or hidden is highly remarkable. This proceeds from the extreme acuteness of their external senses of smell, sight, and taste. Hence, when cattle, sheep, or horses have been stolen, if a native be employed, without much time being allowed to elapse, he can, in general, trace the thieves as well as the stolen property, with the greatest precision, for hundreds of miles; or if any stolen property be hidden for the purpose of avoiding immediate detection, and of being subsequently removed at convenience, a native seldom fails in tracing and finding it wherever it is concealed.

In a remote part of the colony of Victoria, in the year 1851, Mr F——, a stockholder, had occasion to go from his station to Melbourne, distant from a hundred and fifty to two hundred miles. His way for a number of miles lay through his own run, where there were, at considerable distances from each other, huts occupied by his shepherds. He travelled on horseback, starting early in the morning, as is the practice in Australia during the hot season, and carried a large sum of money, a circumstance which happened to be known to his own servants.

On the morning after his departure his family were thrown into a state of alarm by finding that his horse had returned home, and was standing at the stable-door without the rider, the saddle, or bridle. A party immediately set out in quest of Mr F——, but as no trace of him could be found, they returned home. The horse tracks were observed to near the confines of his own lands, but beyond this no mark or trace could be discovered. It thus appeared that the horse had not gone beyond the boundary of Mr F——'s own run, whatever became of himself, his saddle, or bridle. The road which he was discovered to have taken passed close to a hut, near to the boundary of the run, in which two of his own shepherds resided. They stated, on being asked, that they had not seen their master or the horse pass, and knew nothing of him.

In this state of matters, a native, who was occasionally employed as a labourer about the station, volunteered his services to assist the searching party in finding out what had become of Mr F——. The party accordingly resumed their search, accompanied by the native, who traced the horse's track with great dexterity, scanning with his eye, and now and then applying his nose to, the ground. After passing the shepherd's hut already referred to, near the boundary of the run, he made a new discovery. He observed that, besides the horse's track, there were the tracks of two men. His eye at once discovered certain additional derangement of the grass, and, on applying his nose, said, "*Two white mans walk here.*" On proceeding ten or twelve yards further, he again stopped, and, going from side to side of their course, he exclaimed in a state of great excitement, "*Here fight!—here large fight!*" On examining the spot, the grass had evidently been pressed down as if by several men's feet. A few paces further on the native again stopped, and after first looking at the ground, and then applying his nose, exclaimed, in a state of still higher excitement, "*Here kill!—here kill!*" The spot was minutely examined, and on removing some loose earth and sods which had evidently been newly placed there, a great quantity of clotted blood was found. The whole male servants on the run—more than a dozen in number—were with the searching party, and, amongst the others, the two shepherds who lived in the hut which Mr F—— had passed near to the limits of the run. Several of the party remarked that these two shepherds appeared much agitated when the above discoveries were made.

It seemed now quite plain that at this spot Mr F—— had been murdered and robbed; but what became of his body, or of his saddle and saddle-bags, the party could not conjecture. The place where the blood was discovered was near a small stream, which formed the boundary of Mr F——'s run; but it did not appear that he or his horse had crossed that stream, or proceeded further in that direction than the place where the blood was discovered.

The party resolved to continue the services of the native in endeavouring to trace the body of Mr F——. In searching about, accordingly, the native discovered certain tracks of several men leading down the side of the small stream bounding the run. By a long period of dry weather the stream was reduced to a tiny size, and was in some places lost in the sand, and apparently dried up. As in most Australian streams, there were here and there creeks or pools of more or less extent, presenting the appearance of a series of ponds, which, from the smallness of the stream, were nearly stagnant. The party proceeded down this stream for upwards of a mile, the native declaring that he saw several men's tracks. The two shepherds referred to endeavoured to dissuade the party from going further, alleging that they had already searched every place in the neighbourhood without finding the body. The native, however, insisted on proceeding. At length, after travelling several miles, they came to some copsewood in a deep hollow, where the stream formed a large pond, apparently of great depth. The native said the men's tracks had ceased to be perceptible beyond the banks of the pond. He, however, went round and round it. On one side there appeared floating, as in most stagnant ponds, a quantity of dark scum, which the breeze had blown towards the margin. The native took up some of this substance in his hand, and, after several times tasting and smelling it, at length said, pointing to the pond, "*White man here.*" Grappling-irons, and spears with lengthened shafts, were speedily procured; a raft was formed of trees, and, after an hour's search, one of the grappling-irons caught something in the bottom of the pond, which, on being brought to the surface, proved to be a large sack, and, on cutting it open, to contain the mangled remains of poor Mr F——. One end of the sack was filled with heavy stones to prevent the body from floating to the surface; and it was found difficult to raise it on account of its great weight.

A short time before the discovery of the blood above referred to, the searching party were joined by a magistrate, and several police constables; and on discovering the blood, and observing the agitation of the two shepherds, suspicion of the latter's guilt was immediately excited. The magistrate, accordingly, accompanied by two constables, dropped unobserved from the party, and went to the shepherds' hut, where a thorough search was made. Before commencing it, however, a very old female, who had been employed to knit stockings, and who had slept in the hut during the past week, was sent off in charge of a constable, to be lodged at some distance, in order to prevent her from being tampered with, in case her evidence should be afterwards required. Nothing calculated to criminate the parties was found within the hut itself; but in a small outhouse, containing a quantity of old timber, was found concealed a coat, and vest, and two pairs of trousers, with stains of blood on all of them, appearing to have been recently received.

A warrant was immediately issued, and the two shepherds were arrested, and examined by the magistrate, with a law-agent to assist them, who advised them to say nothing, but to reserve their statements for the trial. They were then conveyed by an escort to Melbourne prison.

The saddle and its appendages were still undiscovered, and recourse was once more had to the native labourer, whose services had already proved so valuable. He and the party thereupon made a long search in every place within and without the hut, likely to conceal the lost articles, but to no purpose. At length the native discovered, by sight and smell together, the new tracks of two men's feet, proceeding in a northerly direction from the hut. After travelling about a mile, they came to a sequestered spot in a hollow or gully, where a stream seemed to have run in the rainy season, and where was a mass or cairn of large stones. The tracks were traced to a stone on one side of the cairn, where the native asserted he smelt leather. One stone was removed, and then another, when the saddle, saddle-bags, and bridle, were found, carefully wrapped up, and pushed into an open space betwixt two stones. The bags contained £2000 in money, the sum which Mr F—— was conveying to Melbourne, and they remained untouched. The money was doubtless left here for safety and concealment, and that it might be removed at a convenient time.

The body of Mr F—— being thus found and identified, as well as his saddle, bridle, and saddle-bags, and a number of suspicious circumstances being discovered against the two shepherds, who were examined and committed, the trial took place at Melbourne on an early day thereafter. The tracing of Mr F——'s horse-tracks to the neighbourhood of the hut, the marks on the grass of a struggle having taken place, the finding of the clotted blood, and the agitation of the accused, were all proved by several witnesses. The strenuous attempts made by them to dissuade the party from continuing the search for the body, and the finding of the bloody clothes, were next proved. It was also established by several witnesses, that one of the pairs of trousers, and the coat, were worn by the one prisoner the day before the murder, and the remaining pair and the vest were identified by the same witnesses, as having been worn by the other prisoner on the same day. A chemist in Melbourne swore to having analysed the blood on the stained clothes, and to its being human blood, and not that of any inferior animal. This formed a complete answer to an allegation of the prisoners' counsel, that the blood-stains were caused by the blood of sheep, which the prisoners had killed for use. The old female who had resided in the house at the time of the murder, was next examined. She swore that the prisoners had not gone to bed the night before the murder, but had sat up all night watching some person who was to pass the hut. She likewise stated that while awake in bed early in the morning, she heard the noise of a horse's feet passing, and noticed the two prisoners at the same time leave the hut, and that they did not return for some hours. Several of the searching party proved that on their questioning the accused when the search first commenced, the latter said that they had been in bed all night, and had not risen till a late hour in the morning. Another important piece of evidence was that relative to the tracks of feet discovered from the hut of the accused to where the saddle, saddle-bags, and money were found.

After the counsel for the prosecutor and that for the prisoners had respectively addressed the jury, the case was minutely gone into in an able charge by the judge, and the jury returned a unanimous verdict of guilty against both prisoners, who were afterwards executed at Melbourne. One of the prisoners was a ticket-of-leave convict; the other was a deserter from a regiment in England. Such are the characters who compose a great part of the servants of settlers in the Australian colonies.

MISTAKEN IDENTITY.

In Scotland, as in England, nothing is guarded by proprietors with more intense anxiety and determination than their game and fishings. A number of statutes have accordingly been passed for their protection, and to punish poachers. This is effected in a somewhat anomalous way; for game being wild animals (*feræ naturæ*) are not the property of anybody. Hence it is necessary to prosecute the poacher who takes or kills game, not for theft or robbery, but for a trespass. An ordinary trespass by merely walking on the ground of another, is considered in law a very trivial offence, and is punishable by only a small fine. In proceeding against a poacher, however, it is necessary to prosecute him under the statute for trespassing *with intent to take or kill game.* Accordingly, in addition to the simple trespass, it is necessary to prove the intent. This may be done by proving the possession of a gun, the firing of a shot, or beating the cover with a sporting dog, or similar acts.

The amount of fine or length of imprisonment is greater or less according to circumstances. A second offence involves a higher punishment than a first one. Poaching at night after sunset is also much more severely punished by statute, than if committed during the day.

In the east of Scotland a prosecution was raised against Mr F—— B—— for trespassing on the lands of a nobleman whose game was strictly preserved. Mr B—— was the son of an extensive farmer, and was much respected on account of his intelligence and superior attainments. The case accordingly excited much interest in the neighbourhood. The charge was indignantly denied by the defendant, who was defended by an able solicitor. The act of trespass by a man, whom the witnesses saw on the ground, was clearly proved, as was the fact of killing game, by seeing the trespasser shoot and appropriate a partridge. But some difficulty was experienced in proving the identity of the trespasser with the prisoner. It was during the night that the trespass was committed, and though there was moonlight, it was somewhat cloudy, and it was not easy to distinguish the features of the trespasser. One of the keepers, who was examined as a witness, and who passed nearest to the trespasser, swore unqualifiedly that the person who committed the offence was the accused, and that he thoroughly recognised him. Another swore that he thought it was the accused, but could not be perfectly certain. All the witnesses adduced to prove the trespass swore to the fact that the trespasser was dressed in a light gray shooting-coat and vest, dark trousers, and a red neckerchief, with a light coloured wide-awake hat, and that they saw him proceeding in the direction of the residence of the accused's father, and disappear among some copse near the house. Three or four other witnesses proved that the dress spoken to was identically that which the accused had worn for some time previous to the trespass.

If there be any portion of evidence in regard to which witnesses, judges, and juries should exercise more scrupulous caution than any other, it is that which relates to the identity of the accused with the party committing the offence. Want of caution on this point may lead to the most serious and deplorable results. It may consign an innocent party not only to prison, or penal servitude, but even to the gibbet. Two witnesses were adduced on the part of Mr B—— to prove an *alibi*, but both on very material points of the case broke down. The one swore to having seen him at home during a great part of the evening on which the trespass took place, but could not speak to the particular time of the evening when he so saw him. He also swore that he thought he had on a dark coat and vest, but could not say positively. The other witness swore that the accused was at home during the whole evening, but admitted, in cross-examination, that he could not say but he might have been absent during that evening for an hour or an hour and a half, and could recollect nothing of the dress worn by him.

Night-poaching being a grave offence, the case was tried before the sheriff with a jury. The solicitors for the prosecutor and for the defence having respectively addressed the jury, the sheriff next charged them, and being of opinion that the evidence was sufficient to convict the accused, he directed the jury accordingly. The jury thereupon, by a large majority, (a bare majority in Scotland is sufficient to convict,) returned a verdict of guilty against the prisoner, who was thereupon sentenced by the sheriff to three months' imprisonment.

Although, from the high character of the accused, and the estimation in which he was held, two or three of the fifteen jurymen dissented from the others, yet it was generally believed by the public in that quarter of the country that he was guilty. Poaching is usually practised only by the idle and profligate portion of the community, and is considered highly disreputable, more especially night-poaching. The accused, therefore, felt deeply aggrieved and much chagrined at the result. By three months' imprisonment among criminals, he felt that he was stigmatised as a felon, and would cease to hold the respectable position which he had previously maintained. He therefore resolved, on the close of his imprisonment, to leave his native country for ever, and push his fortune in a foreign land. With this view he got a friend to procure for him a situation in a commercial house at the Cape of Good Hope, to which colony he sailed a few weeks after his liberation from prison.

About a month after Mr B—— had sailed for his new home, the two keepers who had seen the act of poaching, and been the principal witnesses at the trial, happened to be in the county town where the trial had taken place, on business of their master. On passing along the street they saw a crowd of people following two police officers, and on coming up they found the officers had a prisoner in custody, whom they were conveying to the county buildings for examination, on a charge, as they were told, of theft of poultry from a farm in a neighbouring parish, and that his name was Hammond. Curiosity led the keepers to approach nearer the prisoner to get a sight of his face. The one who got the first sight of him, and who was the witness who swore decidedly to the identity of B—— with the poacher at the trial, immediately started back and said to his neighbour, the other keeper, "That is the man whom we saw poaching. I now fully recognise him, and it was not Mr B—— at all. Mr B—— was taller and stouter, and I am positive that this is the man." The other keeper on examining him arrived at the same conclusion. He had, when examined at the trial, expressed himself as not fully satisfied that B—— was the man. He merely said that the poacher was like B——, and that he thought it was he, but was not perfectly certain. Both keepers were now convinced that Hammond was the man whom they saw poaching, and not B——. On returning home, they immediately went to the factor on the estate, and informed him of their discovery. The factor instituted a searching investigation, the result of which was that another witness was discovered, who, the night on which the trespass took place, had seen and conversed with Hammond; was informed by him that he (Hammond) was going to the very place where the trespass occurred, to "get a shot;" and that after B——'s trial was over, Hammond, who was greatly amused at the mistake, told him that it was he who had poached and killed the partridge, and that B—— was not there at all. Lastly, Hammond, who was in prison on commitment, awaiting his trial for theft, knowing that he would not be tried for poaching, since a trial had already taken place on the subject, made a full confession that he was guilty of the act of poaching of which B—— had been convicted.

The noble proprietor of the estate was informed of the occurrence, and B——'s father being one of his principal tenants, his lordship became most anxious to do everything in his power to repair the injury which his tenant had sustained. Having, accordingly, obtained the son's address at the Cape of Good Hope, Mr B—— was no less surprised than gratified to receive one morning from Lord ——, his father's landlord, the following letter:—

"DEAR SIR,—It is with much satisfaction,

mingled however with regret at the injury you have sustained, that I have this day received a letter from my factor at ——, informing me of his having procured complete evidence of your entire innocence of the act of night-poaching, of which a conviction was unfortunately obtained against you in November last. The prosecution took place in the ordinary course of business, and the result originated in a pure mistake. I now, however, write to state that I shall be happy to do everything in my power to repair the injustice of which you have accidentally been the victim. I have taken care to give instructions that the fullest publicity be given of the discovery of your innocence throughout the district where you resided. Should you think of returning home, your former position cannot be in the least degree impaired; and it will afford me great pleasure if I can in any manner promote your interests.—I am," &c.

The mercantile house in which B—— had obtained a situation was one of wealth and high standing. He had just begun to be employed in the management of an important department of the business, and, having incurred a considerable expense in making his arrangements to emigrate, he did not incline to return to Scotland. He also felt some repugnance at the idea of returning to a place where he had been subjected to such unmerited degradation. He accordingly wrote to the noble lord, thanking him for his kind communication, and stating his reasons for not at present returning to this country.

After the lapse of some years, Mr B—— became a partner of the house where he had, since his arrival in the colony, been merely a clerk, and speedily realised a large fortune. He married the daughter of a wealthy merchant at the Cape, and soon ranked among the most respectable merchants of that colony. Having in a short time returned with his wife and family to Scotland, and visited his native county, Lord ——, the prosecutor in the poaching case, heard of his return, and, in addition to other attentions paid to him, gave him a grant for life of a right to shoot over a large section of his extensive estate.

Such was the final result of a prosecution which, however bitterly felt at the close of the trial, proved in the end the means of promoting the accused party's wellbeing and happiness beyond his most sanguine hopes.*

* The above narrative is in substance what actually occurred some years ago, though not in the east of Scotland. The gentleman who was the temporary victim of the prosecution is still in life. He visits Scotland periodically, and enjoys the right of shooting above referred to.

THE FALSE CONSPIRACY.

Mr James O—— was a respectable commission-agent and house-factor in the town of Dundee. In the latter capacity he had charge of a great number of tenements of houses in different parts of the town, including the letting of these to tenants, removing of tenants, and collecting the rents. Among others, there was a house in a retired and somewhat mean part of the town, let to a Mrs Turnley, who followed the occupation of a broker, dealing in articles of dress, pieces of old furniture, and miscellaneous articles. She did not bear a peculiarly high character, and was reputed to be occasionally addicted to inebriety; but she was young, and somewhat attractive in appearance. Being considerably in arrear of rent, Mr O—— sent her notice that he would call at twelve o'clock the Friday following for payment of the rent, and intimated that unless payment of the arrears were made, he would be compelled by his employer's instructions to apply for a sequestration, and remove her from the premises. He called accordingly, but soon after entering the house a great noise and struggle was heard, and loud cries by Mrs Turnley. Three men, who were drinking in a small public-house in the neighbourhood, kept by a Mrs Dale, hearing the cries, came to her assistance, and found her lying on the floor with her hair all dishevelled, her dress in disorder and partly torn, and James O—— beside her. There were several marks of blood on her face and neck, and a small shawl or handkerchief which she had on her neck was stained and saturated with blood. Two police-constables were sent for, but the case was of such a nature that it was at once placed in the hands of the procurator-fiscal, with an information on the part of Mrs Turnley, apparently calculated in every way to found a charge of assault with intent to ravish. The procurator-fiscal, however, proceeded with great caution. He knew the character of Mr O—— to be highly respectable, while there was an odour in regard to that of Mrs Turnley of a tendency in some measure the reverse. He therefore tested all the evidence tendered by Mrs Turnley with the greatest care; and, on the other hand, he gave every facility to Mr O—— to prepare his defence. After the usual examination before the sheriff, Mr O—— was committed for trial for the crime of assault with intent to ravish, but he was admitted to bail. Mrs Turnley at the same time raised a civil action for reparation against Mr O—— before the Sheriff Court.

Mr O——'s trial came on before the Court of Justiciary soon after his commitment. The indictment charged him with assaulting Mrs Turnley to the effusion of blood, and serious injury of her person, and that with intent to ravish her. The prisoner pleaded not guilty. The facts of the case will be best gathered from the short epitome of the evidence as given on the trial.

Mrs Turnley was first sworn and examined. She said, "I follow the occupation of a broker, and live in —— Street of Dundee. I occupy a house there, for the proprietor of which the prisoner is factor. The prisoner occasionally comes to my house for the payment of rent, and regarding other matters connected with the house. He was there on Friday the 20th February last, for the purpose of getting payment of some rent which was due by me. After entering the house he began to use liberties with me, and made an indecent proposal, which I indignantly rejected, cautioning him that he must behave himself properly. He thereupon seized hold of me, and threw me down violently on the floor, attempting most improper conduct. I struggled with all my might to put him off me, and called aloud for assistance. At length three men, who happened to be in a public-house in the neighbourhood, came to my assistance, and I was rescued. My dress was torn; I was wounded in the neck and arms, and lost a great deal of blood." Examined for the prisoner, she said, "I cannot shew the marks of the wounds on my neck and arms, as they are healed up. I got no blood whatever from a butcher on the night of Thursday the 19th, or morning of Friday the 20th of February, or at any other time. I may have been in Mrs Dale's house the forenoon of the day when Mr O—— called. I may have seen there, and spoken to the three men who afterwards came to my rescue." (Admonished by the prisoner's counsel.) "Recollect you are upon oath; I do not ask whether you *may* have been there—but, were you or were you not in Mrs Dale's house, and did you see and converse with these three men?" Witness: "I was in Mrs Dale's house, and saw the three men there." Prisoner's counsel: "Did you sit in company with them and partake of spirits?" Witness: "That is an improper question; it is nothing to you what I did." Presiding judge: "You must answer the question, it is of importance." Witness: "I think I did speak to them, and partook of some of their whisky." Prisoner's counsel: "Did you pay for the whisky?" Witness: "I do not recollect." Question repeated. "I think I did pay something." Prisoner's counsel: "Did you pay for all the whisky they had?" Witness: "I am not sure, I paid for some of it." Prisoner's counsel: "Did you arrange with these men that they were to call on you about twelve o'clock, and to go up when they heard loud cries by you?" Witness: "No, I made no arrangement whatever."

The three men who were in Mrs Dale's house, and came to Mrs Turnley's on hearing her cries, were next examined. They all three confirmed her statements as to the condition in which she was when they entered her house—with her dress torn, bleeding profusely, and the prisoner on the top of her, holding her down. But while one of the men admitted, on cross-examination, after being pressed, that Mrs Turnley was in his and that of the other two men's company, and drinking spirits with them in Mrs Dale's public-house, the other two denied that they had seen her that day, until they went to her own house, in consequence of hearing loud cries of distress.

Great suspicions were thus cast upon the last three witnesses, by their contradiction of each other respecting their meeting with Mrs Turnley; and not a little suspicion was attracted to the evidence of Mrs Turnley herself, owing to the evasive answers which she gave, and her extreme reluctance in giving them. The following exculpatory evidence was next led on the part of the prisoner:—

James Steedman, sworn and examined, said, "I am a butcher in —— Street of Dundee. My shop is in the immediate neighbourhood of the house of Mrs Turnley, whom I see here to-day. I remember of hearing, one day in February last, that Mrs Turnley was attacked that forenoon in her house, and maltreated by Mr O——. I went to her house and saw her, and she had all the appearance of a person who had been attacked. Her dress was out of order and torn, and some stains of blood were upon her arms, hands, and neck. The night before this attack took place, I recollect of her coming to my shop with an empty bottle, and asking for some blood. I had no blood in the shop, but I sent and got it for her. I wondered what she was going to make of a bottle of blood, and I asked her for what she wanted it, but I do not remember what she said. I charged nothing for it, as she was a customer."

Mrs Isabel Dale, sworn and examined, said, "I keep a public-house in —— Street, next door to Mrs Turnley's house. I remember of three men coming into my house in February last, between ten and eleven o'clock in the forenoon. Mrs Turnley was along with them. She called for half-a-mutchkin of whisky, and treated them. She also took part of it herself. She then called for more whisky. I wondered what business they were going to transact, as they were talking in whispers. After taking the whisky she spoke louder, and, as I was sitting in a room adjoining the one they were in, and to which there was a door leading to their apartment, I heard what passed. I overheard Mrs Turnley say, 'I will do for him; I will pull him on the top of me, and keep a hold of him, and cry as loud as I can. Run you up then, and you will see him upon me.'" This piece of evidence created a great sensation in court. "I did not understand at the time what she meant. I thought it was some acquaintance she meant to play a trick upon for their amusement. She then added, 'I will let him off, if he gives down all the rent, and pays me £5.' She also said, 'I have got some blood to sprinkle myself with, and they will think he treated me with great violence.' After I heard what had taken place in Mrs Turnley's house the same day, and that Mr O—— was taken into custody, and to be tried, I knew at once what the conversation in my house meant; I now saw plainly that Mrs Turnley and those three men had made up a plan to bring a false charge against Mr O——, with the view of extorting money, and that she might get quit of her rent. I knew Mr O—— was much respected in the place, and I thought it a most abominable affair."

Mr A——, surgeon and chemist, was next examined. He said, "I am a surgeon and chemist. I am accustomed to analyse chemically, and have much experience in chemistry. I examined minutely the small shawl on the table, labelled as belonging to Mrs Turnley, and a number of deep stains of blood thereon. I applied a powerful microscope to these different stains, and I can swear decidedly that the blood thereon is the blood of a cow or some other inferior animal, and is not human blood. The globules composing human blood are entirely different from those in the blood of the inferior animals." Here the foreman of the jury interfered, and said the jury were unanimously of opinion that they need not trouble the court any further, and that there was not only no evidence against the prisoner, but that there was complete evidence of his entire innocence. They therefore begged to return a verdict of not guilty; and they at the same time took the opportunity to express their great abhorrence at the conduct of the witnesses for the Crown, who had plainly entered into a foul conspiracy for the purpose of destroying the character of a respectable and innocent man. After a suitable address from the judge, expressive of his entire concurrence with the opinion of the jury, and informing the prisoner that he would leave the bar without the smallest stain on his character, he was dismissed from the bar.

Immediately after the intimation by the jury, the

judge told the public prosecutor that he ought to cause the four Crown witnesses to be taken into custody, judicially examined, and, if necessary, committed for trial. This course seemed so palpably necessary, that the advocate-depute had sent for the procurator-fiscal, and got the complaint and warrant prepared before the judge had made the suggestion. Mrs Turnley and her three accomplices were accordingly examined, and committed for trial on the grave charge of false conspiracy.

The trial for false conspiracy having come soon afterwards before the Court of Justiciary, it was of short duration. Mr O—— himself was the leading witness, and was followed by Steedman the butcher, Mrs Dale, the public-house-keeper, and the medical witness who proved the nature of the blood on Mrs Turnley's shawl. The three last witnesses simply repeated the evidence they had already given on Mr O——'s trial. The only new evidence, therefore, was that of Mr O—— himself, and which was to the following effect:—"I sent notice to Mrs Turnley that I would call on Friday following, the 20th February, at twelve o'clock, for payment of her arrears of rent, and that if these were not paid, I would be obliged to sequestrate and remove her. I called, accordingly, and found her extremely complaisant. She said I was a great stranger—that she would be glad if I would call oftener; and said, in a half whisper, she would be much pleased if I would come up and stay all night, and she would make me comfortable—it would be so nice. I said to her I had no taste for such things. She said she must give me a taste. She then put her arms round my neck, and began to kiss me, which I resisted; upon which she, suddenly falling on the floor, pulled me on the top of her, and immediately called out murder, and for help. I thought she had become mad, either with excessive drinking or otherwise. I never thought of a conspiracy till I saw the three men enter the apartment. I then saw at once that Mrs Turnley and they were acting in concert. One said, seizing hold of me, 'What blackguard conduct to a decent woman! You'll be hanged!' Another said, 'We'll take you to the jail.' The third said, 'See the blood on the poor woman, from your knocking her about.' On looking, I was quite astonished to see a great deal of blood on her neck, and her shawl all stained. I knew there was no violence at all, except what she herself created by pulling me on the top of her; and I could not understand where the blood came from. I was so much taken by surprise that I could hardly believe my own senses. I never before met with such daring conduct. I was almost unable to say anything from utter surprise, and from not seeing at the time the object in view. The men said they would go for the police. I, however, observed Mrs Turnley motioning to them to leave the room, and they left, accordingly; but I observed that they went into an adjoining room. She then said to me in a whisper, 'If you give me down all my rent, and pay me £5, there will be nothing more about this.' I told her I would neither give down nor pay her one farthing; that she and these blackguards might do their worst. She then went ont of the room, bringing back two of the men, and a third went and brought two police constables, who took me into custody."

Mr Steedman, Mrs Dale, and the medical practitioner being next examined, gave the same evidenc as in the former trial. The jury, as was done b the other jury on the trial of Mr O——, at th close of the evidence of the medical witness, inte posed, and declared themselves fully satisfied wit the evidence already given as amply sufficient t convict the four prisoners, unless the latter had an exculpatory evidence. The prisoners' counsel, wh saw from the outset that his labour was in vai stated that he had no exculpatory evidence to ac duce. The jury thereupon returned a verdict c guilty against all the prisoners.

The judge, in pronouncing sentence, addresse the prisoners in the strongest terms. He remarke as follows:—"It is wholly out of my power t embody in language anything at all calculated pr perly to characterise the enormity of the crime yo have committed. You all four banded yourselve together for the purpose of utterly ruining th character and position of a respectable man, an consigning him to infamy and disgrace. If suc conduct were permitted, no individual, howeve irreproachable his character or elevated his pos tion, would be safe for a single moment. He might in a single day be utterly degraded, and classed with the lowest of felons. It would be a state of things whereby society would be utterly unhinged by the most wicked, unprincipled system of wholesale fraud and perjury. The sentence of the court is, that all of you be sent to penal servitude for ten years from this date." *

* This is substantially the report of a case which occurred some years ago, and was tried in the Court of Justiciary; but Dundee was not the scene of the transaction.

THE DEAD REVIVED

About the beginning of the present century, th owner of a fishing-smack in Eyemouth, engage in the herring and mackerel-fishing, sent Josep Ridgeby, Edward Ferrie, and John Brown, th three hands composing the crew, one evening, to distance of seven or eight miles, to fish for mackere The night was dark, and therefore highly favour able for net-fishing, a clear night being always con sidered unfavourable, enabling the fish to see th net and avoid its meshes. Like many of the fisher men on that coast, Ridgeby and Ferrie were mucl addicted to inebriety, and although, like the rest o their brethren, they received large wages, the whol were usually expended by them in drink. The consequence was that they were usually in debt, and pressed for money. Brown, on the contrary, was a sober, steady man, and never in straitened circumstances. He had that afternoon received from his master twelve pounds of wages. The other two observing that he had received that sum, immediately applied to him for a loan. He was perfectly aware, in the first place, that whatever sum he gave them would be expended in drink, and in the next, that if he complied with their request, he never would again see a farthing of the loan. He therefore refused their request, alleging that he had himself occasion for the money. Both Ridgeby and Ferrie were much disappointed and exasperated, as they had urgent demands upon them for certain monies that very morning. Having failed to induce Brown to lend the money, and observing that he had the amount received by him in a pocket-book which he carried in his side-pocket, and had with him while going on board the smack to proceed to the fishing-ground, they secretly devised the wicked scheme of robbing him after getting out to sea, and of afterwards murde ing him to prevent detection. Ferrie at firs though he agreed to the robbery, objected strong to the murder, proposing to leave Brown in son place where he might be picked up by a vess bound for a foreign port, and so be prevented fro returning to Eyemouth. Ridgeby pointed out th this course was unsuitable, as they could not ca culate on a vessel bound for a foreign port passi in their course, and would not in a dark night s what description of vessels did so. Brown, mor over, could not in any event, if left alive, fail find his way back to Eyemouth, when the robbe would be at once divulged, and they prosecuted a punished. In these circumstances, Ferrie at leng consented to be a coadjutor in the murder as w as in the robbery. Accordingly, after reaching t fishing-ground eight miles distant, and shooti and drawing the nets several times, and bringi in some considerable hauls of mackerel, Ridgeb who, as well as Ferrie, had fortified his resoluti by large potations of gin, commenced to pick quarrel with Brown for refusing the loan, and w joined by Ferrie. Ridgeby next taking up the tiller, dealt him a severe blow, intended for his head, but which, by his partly avoiding it, fell upon his shoulder. Brown, at length, considering that his antagonists, who were both very powerful men, would easily overpower him, and perceiving that they intended either to murder him or do him very serious injury, entreated them to spare his life, and he would give them all he was possessed of. He immediately pulled out his pocket-book, containing the twelve pounds, his watch, and a purse, in which he had a quantity of silver, and laid the whole before them. Upon this, Ridgeby, having his knife in readiness for the purpose, and strongly impressed with the truth of the saying that dead men tell no tales, gave him a thrust with it in the side with great force. On this, Brown exclaimed, "O God, you have done for me at last!" and fell to the bottom of the boat. Both his antagonists then took hold of him for the purpose of throwing him overboard, but perceiving their intention, he cried, "For Heaven's sake let me die in the boat!" His cries were of no avail. They lifted him up, and after looking about them in case any vessel might be near, and finding there was none, threw him into the sea. Having thus disposed of their victim, they immediately set sail and returned with the breeze towards the Berwickshire coast, reaching Eyemouth about two o'clock in the morning. They had thus possessed themselves of upwards of twelve pounds in money and a valuable watch; and having stabbed the owner, mortally, as they supposed, and tossed his body into the Germau Ocean, so far from shore, in a pitch dark night, where he could not save himself, even if he had not been stabbed at all, they felt completely secure from the slightest risk of discovery. They told their master and Brown's friends at Eyemouth that while shooting the nets he had fallen accidentally overboard and been drowned; that owing to the extreme darkness of the night they could not save him, notwithstanding every exertion on their part to do so. Their story was fully credited, and poor Brown's friends and acquaintances lamented his death as that of one who had lost his life by an unfortunate accident.

For a week or two after this occurrence, Ridgeby and Ferrie were observed to be more than usually well supplied with money, and to be constantly indulging in evening potations. An intimate friend of Brown, whom Ridgeby had one evening treated in a tavern to some whisky-toddy, remarked on seeing him take out his pocket-book to pay the reckoning, that that pocket-book belonged to poor Brown. Ridgeby said, with some confusion, that it resembled Brown's, but was not his. It had several unmistakeable distinctive marks, however, which Brown's friend at once noticed, and by which he recognised it as the property of Brown. About the same time, a friend of Ferrie's landlady, who was also an intimate associate of Brown, happening to be one evening in the landlady's house when Ferrie was not at home, was asked to go into the apartment where the latter slept, to see a new watch, which she said he had got. He did so, and instantly recognised the watch as Brown's. It immediately became known to every person in Eyemouth that Ridgeby and Ferrie were in possession of Brown's pocket-book and watch, and to have a much larger supply of money than usual. These discoveries could not fail to excite the gravest suspicions. It seemed obvious to every one that if Brown was drowned by accidentally falling overboard as was stated, his watch and pocket-book must have been lost with him. He could not, under any circumstances, be supposed to have taken them off his person in an open fishing-smack, in a dark night. Every one was therefore strongly impressed with the belief that Brown must have been robbed and then murdered. These suspicions were in no way allayed by Ridgeby and Ferrie, both asserting that the watch and pocket-book were not the property of Brown at all, though several persons had, on the contrary, fully recognised them as having belonged to him at the time he met with his death. The general aspect of the whole affair finally determined Brown's relations to lodge an information with one of the procurators-fiscal of the sheriff-court of Berwickshire.

A full investigation was immediately instituted by the procurator-fiscal, who speedily came to Eyemouth for the purpose of taking a precognition.

It is remarkable on how improved a footing a case is placed by professional experience and systematic procedure, compared with the aspect it assumes when it only rests on the loose inquiries of a private party. The procurator-fiscal, after apprehending Ridgeby and Ferrie on a sheriff's warrant, and examining them, obtained a remand for further examination. He also got a warrant to search for the watch and pocket-book, which he accordingly recovered. He next examined the friend of the deceased John Brown, who observed the pocket-book in the possession of Ridgeby, and obtained a complete description of the characteristic marks by which it was identified. He explained that the pocket-book was of a purple colour, that the strap which surrounded and closed it, had been partially broken off, and the part so removed was replaced by another portion of strap, black in the colour, and clumsily fastened on with light-coloured thongs. He also identified the watch as that of the deceased. It was still more thoroughly identified by the watch-maker at Eyemouth who sold it to Brown, and spoke to its number, and description, and the maker's name. Several fishermen were examined, who saw Brown with the watch upon him about half-an-hour before going on board the smack. The prisoners were next judicially examined a second time. Ridgeby denied positively that the pocket-book belonged to Brown. He said it was bought by himself in Edinburgh some years before. Ferrie, in his declaration, also denied that the watch was Brown's, and said that he bought it lately before, from an English fisherman whom he met in Berwick-upon-Tweed. Both prisoners were finally committed for trial.

After the commitment of the two prisoners, several important discoveries were made by the public prosecutor. In particular, it was discovered that both prisoners made different payments to merchants in Eyemouth the day after Brown's disappearance; while several witnesses proved that they had no money two days before, and could not meet the claims of debt that were made against them. A five-pound note was discovered which Ridgeby had paid to a merchant in Eyemouth to whom he owed an account; and his master, the owner of the smack, declared on precognition, that it was one of the notes forming part of the twelve pounds which he had paid to Brown. The suspicions being very strong against the prisoners that they had murdered Brown in order to prevent detection of the robbery, the warrant of commitment was obtained on the alternative charges of murder, robbery, or theft. The solicitor, however, into whose hands they placed their case, informed them that he was decidedly of opinion that the charge of murder could not be proved against them, even if they had committed such a crime, as, without the production of Brown's body, or other very strong evidence, the *corpus delicti*, as it is called in law language—that is, the fact of any murder at all having been committed—could not possibly be established. But he told them that, by the law of Scotland, any person finding the property of another, and keeping possession of, or using it without delivering it up, is held to be guilty of theft. Being thoroughly convinced, therefore, that Brown was safe in the bottom of the sea, and that beyond the possession of the money and articles referred to, there was not a tittle of evidence against them, they felt perfectly secure against every charge except that of theft, and even that of a mitigated kind. In the meantime, the procurator-fiscal discovered some most extraordinary testimony—as unexpected by him as it was by the accused—which will be noticed in the sequel.

The prisoners were tried before the Court of Justiciary. In the indictment served upon them, they were surprised to find that the charge of murder was abandoned, and that instead of it was substituted that of aggravated assault, with intent to murder, and to the effusion of blood and danger of life. They were also charged with robbery of the watch, pocket-book, and money. They imagined, however, that the charge of murder was abandoned merely because the body could not be found; and they considered any attempt to prove an assault equally hopeless as that to establish a murder. The trial having come on, their counsel finding that there would be a complete identification of the watch, advised them to admit that it was

Brown's property, but that they had found it on board the smack where he had laid it. They denied that the money and pocket-book were his, and asserted that they belonged to Ridgeby. Defences having been lodged to this effect, and a jury empannelled, a great many witnesses were examined to prove the identity of the different articles, and particularly of the notes, several of which, besides the five-pound note, were recovered, traced to the prisoners, and proved to have belonged to Brown. A long list of witnesses was appended to the indictment; but the prisoners and their counsel paid little regard to it, being satisfied that they could only be adduced to prove the identity of the money and other articles. To a great extent this was the case, as nearly the whole list was composed of witnesses brought forward with this view. At length a witness was called near the end of the list. A thin, pale figure advanced towards the witness-box. There were a number of Eyemouth people in court, many of whom had been examined as witnesses at the previous part of the trial, and had now mixed with the audience. Others had attended from curiosity to hear the proceedings. No sooner had the light fallen on the face of the pale figure who was entering the witness-box, than an exclamation of surprise, followed by a shout of applause, burst from a large portion of the spectators when they saw, *in propria persona,* John Brown, the man supposed by all but the public prosecutor to have been murdered as well as robbed. Had a thunderbolt struck the prisoners, they could not have been more astounded or appalled. Ferrie fainted away, and Ridgeby became deadly pale. Their counsel was taken completely by surprise. The name of John Brown, residing in a street in London, among a numerous list of witnesses, never drew his attention, the name being one so very common; and it was a perfectly settled point in their minds that John Brown of Eyemouth was long since drowned and dead.

Ferrie being restored to consciousness by the aid of cold water, and Brown being sworn and examined at great length, gave his evidence with much clearness. After relating the attempt by the prisoners to borrow money from him, the subsequent quarrel which they fastened on him, the blow with the tiller, the delivery by the witness of his money and watch, the stab by Ridgeby, and of both having seized and thrown him overboard, as noticed before, he gave evidence as follows: — "When thrown into the sea the night was very dark, and the boat from which I was thrown immediately disappeared from my view. I was weak from loss of blood, but managed to float on my back for some time. In about ten minutes I felt something touching me, and grasping it with great eagerness, I found it was a large plank of wood. I managed, by great exertion, first to get my breast and body placed upon it, and afterwards to sit on it, with a leg on each side. I then got a cravat from my pocket, which I tied firmly round my body, so as to prevent, if possible, the flow of blood from my wound. In about half-an-hour after getting on the plank, the night became clear, and I soon observed the disc of the moon rising above the horizon. To my unspeakable joy, I observed a sail some miles distant, which I noticed was coming in my direction. I at length called as loud as I could, but for some time I was unheard. At last, when about a mile distant, I was heard, and a cry was made in answer. I soon thereafter saw a boat with four oars advancing. I was picked up and taken on board the ship, which proved to be the *Hope* of London, from Cronstadt, bound to the former port with a cargo of goods. I was treated with great kindness by the master, who furnished me with dry clothes, gave me hot negus, and put me to bed. My wound was examined and dressed by a surgeon who was on board. He said the wound was deep, but not dangerous, though, had the knife not met with many obstructions, which diverted the course of the thrust, it would certainly have been fatal. The thick, tough clothing which the knife had to penetrate, weakened to a great extent the force of the thrust, and, the point of the knife having glanced on one of the ribs, was diverted to the fleshy part of the side, which it entered, without penetrating the internal part of the body. The tight bandage of a cravat round my waist, coupled with the coldness of the night, he said, had stopped the flow of blood from my wound, otherwise I might have perished from loss of blood. In about a week the ship arrived in London. From the weakness caused by the loss of blood, and the intense cold which I endured, a fever ensued, and I was sent to Bethlehem Hospital, from which, by careful and attentive nursing and skilful treatment, I was able to remove in about six or seven weeks. I only left the hospital about ten days ago."

The surgeon and master of the *Hope* were also examined, who confirmed Brown's testimony in every particular. The former spoke to the dangerous state of the wound, and the condition in which he was picked up.

Brown was listened to with the most intense interest by the audience, the court, and the jury. The jury were addressed by the advocate-depute for the Crown, followed by the counsel for the prisoner. The presiding judge next addressed the jury in a clear and luminous charge, minutely analysing the whole evidence. The jury returned a verdict finding the prisoners guilty of robbery as libelled, and of assault to the serious injury of the person, danger of life, and with intent to murder.

In awarding the punishment of transportation, the judge addressed the prisoners as follows:— "Joseph Ridgeby and Edward Ferrie, after a long, protracted trial, you have, by a most respectable jury, and evidence as clear as could be adduced in any case, been found guilty of the crimes of robbery and most aggravated assault, with intent to murder. The circumstances of your case are such as I cannot find language sufficiently strong to express my abhorrence of, and to stigmatise as it deserves. In point of unprincipled wickedness, atrocious, cold-blooded, and heartless cruelty, it finds no parallel in any case that has ever come before me. The innocent and unsuspecting object of your dreadful schemes was your own associate and fellow-servant. The end to be gained was to possess yourselves of his hard-earned wages, of which and his watch you first robbed him. Then one of you, with a sharp knife, wielded with determined force, inflicted a severe wound, intended to deprive him of life. In this helpless, maimed, and apparently dying state, both of you next seized and threw him overboard, where you left him to perish in the dead hour of night in the depths of the ocean, far from land and from the chance of rescue. But a more powerful arm than yours was then present. The deadly weapon was diverted from its course. Though consigned to the deep, and beyond the verge of human hope, he was sustained and preserved in a most providential manner, and brought to a safe asylum, where, by kind and skilful treatment, he has been restored to health, and placed here this day to confront you—scattering your false statements to the winds, and laying open to the light of day your fiendish plans for his destruction. Luckily for you, a change has taken place in the law of punishments, else you could not have escaped the extreme penalty of death. As it is, the highest punishment which the law allows shall be inflicted, namely, that you be transported beyond seas for the whole period of your natural lives."

THE STOLEN HEIRESS.

CHILD-STEALING, termed "plagium" in the Roman law, has always been viewed and treated by the law of Scotland as the most aggravated species of theft, and was formerly punished uniformly with death. The loss by theft of a living object, on whom a parent has centred his or her fondest affections, is an afflicting wrong, the extent of which none but a parent can estimate.

Mr Campbell of ——, a proprietor in the west of Scotland, had a daughter, an only child on whom he and his wife set their warmest affections. She was a little past two years of age, could speak and prattle, and climb eagerly on the knees of her parents in quest of the much-valued kiss. These and other engaging acts made little Cecilia the idol of her parents. The latter went one Sunday morning to attend worship in an Episcopal chapel situated at a considerable distance from home, leaving two female servants in the house, the one being the nursery-maid, whom they left in charge of their little darling daughter, and the other in charge of the house. The remaining servants were attending the Presbyterian services in the parish church two or three miles distant, from which they did not return till the termination of the afternoon service. Mr and Mrs Campbell did not return for several hours afterwards. On their return they were amazed on ringing the door-bell for some time to gain no admission. At length the cook made her appearance in a state of great agitation. She informed them that the nursery-maid had gone to walk with little Cecilia in the forenoon, and while speaking with some acquaintance whom she met on the road, her little charge had disappeared, and she could not find her after the most anxious search. The housemaid and she had searched every place they could think of, and been joined in the search by all the other servants on their return from church; and they must be still engaged in the search, as none of them had returned since they had joined the nursery-maid and house-maid. The intelligence operated like a thunderbolt on poor Mrs Campbell, who fainted away. On her husband, whose nervous system was more powerful, though equally appalled by the intelligence, the effect was different. On seeing his wife properly attended to, he instantly left the house, roused all the inhabitants in the neighbourhood, including those of a neighbouring fishing village, who searched every place for a number of miles round, but without success. It baffled all their endeavours to find the slightest trace of little Cecilia. There was no place of great danger in the neighbourhood where she could have been lost, and no pool, pond, or stream, into which she could have fallen without her body being at once found. Even had she been run over and killed, or injured by any carriage or horse on the public road, her remains could not fail to be at once discovered. The decided conclusion come to, therefore, by Mr Campbell and every one engaged in the search, was that she must have been stolen and carried off by some person or other passing along the road. It was ascertained on inquiry that the acquaintance who had engaged the nursery-maid's attention, was a male admirer who was in the habit of visiting her, with whom she had walked in a wood for a considerable time, leaving Cecilia alone near the public road, where she lay amusing herself with some flowers, and on returning about half-an-hour or more afterwards to take her home, she was nowhere to be seen. Mr Campbell accordingly became satisfied that his little daughter must have been stolen by some person passing along the public road, but by whom such a daring act was performed he could not conjecture. The search, which was carried on for a number of hours by several hundred persons of every age, was active and most anxious, now terminated by darkness, and Mr Campbell with a sore heart returned home to tell his wife that their darling child had not been found.

By the earliest glimmering of dawn next morning, Mr Campbell was mounted on horseback. His own horses and every other on the estate were put in requisition. All his servants, with his whole tenants and their servants, turned out to renew the search of the preceding day. There were three different roads which it was considered necessary to pursue in order to ensure success in the search. Of these, two led towards the Firth of Clyde, and one in an easterly direction. Mr Campbell himself, with about a dozen of mounted attendants, took the most frequented of the two former, while other two sections of the party took each one of the other two roads. It was ascertained that a numerous party of tinkers or gipsies, with donkies, had passed along the road near Mr Campbell's house the day before, during the forenoon church service. They consequently became convinced that the tinkers must have stolen the child while the nursery-maid had so culpably left her alone near the public road. They further ascertained that the gipsies had separated into two parties after passing Mr Campbell's residence, and that the foremost party had travelled at a much quicker rate than the other. This was another suspicious circumstance. Mr Campbell and his party accordingly pushed on with all the speed in their power, and received information at different places as they went along that the two parties of gipsies had passed in that direction the evening before. At length Mr Campbell overtook, in the course of the afternoon, the last or rear party of the gipsies in the neighbourhood of Greenock. They were six or seven in number, and had two donkies and four or five children; but little Cecilia was not among them, as they found after a thorough search. They seemed to give a prompt and distinct account of all their proceedings the day before. They admitted at once that they came from the north of Argyleshire, and had passed Mr Campbell's residence the day before, early in the forenoon, that they were then in company with another party of tinkers or gipsies, who had parted with them, having gone on before and travelled with dispatch for the purpose of overtaking and attending some market in the east of Scotland. But they denied having seen any of their party take a child from the road-side, or from any place in their route, or that they saw any child whatever of the description mentioned. They also expressed much surprise at the theft of such a child being suspected, as they said they did not think any one would dare to commit such an offence, especially on the child of a gentleman of rank. Mr Campbell was, however, resolved to overtake the party who had gone towards the east, and having dismissed all the party who accompanied him except his own servants, he proceeded towards Glasgow, communicating with the county police at different stations. Several parties of gipsies or tinkers were found in Lanarkshire, and between that and Edinburgh, but all of them denied having been in the direction of Mr Campbell's residence; and though they were all searched, no child of the description of little Cecilia was found in their company. The chief constables of all the towns and counties were communicated with, and enjoined to make every investigation, and to offer rewards of large amount for the recovery of the child. Advertisements describing her, and offering large rewards, were inserted in all the principal newspapers in Scotland and England, but all without any result. A superintendent of police at Greenock had given information that a party of tinkers or gipsies had been seen entering a steamer for the coast of Ireland at an early hour one morning about the time when the child was missed; but the father paid no attention to the information, conceiving it perfectly out of the question that any child could be stolen in Scotland, for the purpose of being conveyed to Ireland, where hundreds of children would be parted with gratuitously to any person who would maintain them. After making every effort that could be thought of for many successive months, without the slightest trace of his little daughter being discovered, the father, with a heavy heart, was obliged to abandon the work as hopeless. The poor mother, after being in a state of mind approaching to distraction, sunk into a state of fixed melancholy. All hope of meeting the darling object of her affections in this world having vanished, she cherished only the hope of doing so in the regions of eternal bliss.

Mrs Campbell's state of mind having induced delicate health, her husband found it necessary every summer to take her on some excursion, with the view, if possible, to divert her mind from the bitter reflections consequent on her sad bereavement. These excursions were varied every year, in order that novelty of scene and objects might aid his intentions. Nearly ten years elapsed from the time of the child's loss, wheu chance directed them one summer on an excursion to the north and west of Ireland. The weather was very fine, and the scenery in that quarter, always beautiful, was that season peculiarly attractive. After passing through the north, and part of the west of Ireland, they entered the county of Fermanagh. By travelling one or two stages longer than usual, in passing through the county of Donegal, Mrs Campbell became over-fatigued, and found it necessary to rest for some days at the first suitable hotel or inn they could find. Having, therefore, found an extremely neat and clean stage inn, near the foot of Loch Erne, they resolved to sojourn there for a week. Besides being a stage inn, it was much frequented by anglers and other sportsmen. The provisions and beds were both excellent, and the attendance extremely good. Mrs Campbell directed that she should be supplied each morning and evening with warm milk fresh from the cow. The landlady arranged, accordingly, with a respectable farmer in the neighbourhood, who supplied the inn with milk and other provisions, to send the supply of milk required. The young female who brought it went with it direct to Mrs Campbell's room. She was apparently about twelve years of age, elegant in figure, and exquisitely beautiful. There was something in her appearance and manner that attracted Mrs Campbell's attention to her in a way she could not explain. She remarked this to her own maid, an old servant, who had been long in her employment, and who said that was precisely her own feeling. She added that she could not help remarking that her face, in some of its features, bore a strong resemblance to the pretty face of little Cecilia. As her style and dress were superior to that of a common servant, Mrs Campbell asked her on her next visit if she was the daughter of Mr Monigail (the farmer who supplied the milk.) She answered, in a somewhat embarrassed manner, that she was not,—she was his niece. She then added, with great naïveté, "At least, Mrs Monigail calls me her niece; but, in reality, I am no relation of Mr and Mrs Monigail. I am an orphan. My father and mother, as I understand, are both dead. I came from Scotland when I was a child of only two years old. Mrs Monigail, who has no family of her own, has brought me up and educated me as her own daughter, and treats me with the utmost kindness."

After her departure, Mrs Campbell, who was much excited by what she heard about her having come from Scotland when a child, now expressed her belief that Eliza Monigail (the name given to the young milk-maid) was really her daughter Cecilia. Her maid expressed herself still more thoroughly convinced of the fact. "But," said Mrs Campbell, "what proof have we?" "I can ascertain and prove it in one minute," said the old maid. "Don't you remember that little Cecilia had a large mole on her right side, of the size and form of a plum; and she also had on her back, near the spine, two peculiar-looking moles close to each other, one large, and of a round shape; the other smaller, and of an oval shape. These marks are never effaced; and if she has them, she is assuredly no other than Cecilia Campbell." Mrs Campbell clearly remembered the marks, and was delighted at the idea of at once ascertaining whether her conjectures were well founded. Her anxiety was so intense, that she could not wait till Eliza's ordinary visit in the evening, but sent a message to request that she would call in half-an-hour, as she wished to see her. Eliza attended punctually. She was better dressed than when acting the milk-maid, and looked, what she really was, a most lovely girl. Mrs Campbell requested her to be seated, and began to converse with her in presence of her old maid. The former, however, between hope and the fear of disappointment, was so agitated that she could hardly speak. At length, on somewhat recovering her self-possession, she said, in as bland terms as possible, "Eliza, you must not be annoyed at what I am about to ask you, as I have some idea that I have seen you before. May I ask if you have a large mole on your right side, about the size and shape of a plum or large strawberry?" Eliza's countenance, which expressed the utmost surprise, was immediately suffused with a crimson blush. She at length answered, "Yes, ma'am; but I don't understand how you know that." "I will tell you by and by," said Mrs Campbell; "but answer me this one other question, Have you two moles on your back, near the spine?" "Yes, I have indeed," said the astonished girl; "and the one is round, and about the size of a silver penny; the other is smaller, and of an oval shape." Mrs Campbell was perfectly delighted, but asked if she would kindly allow her and her maid to see the marks by undoing her dress; with which request she at once complied. Mrs Campbell and her maid instantly recognised the well-known marks, and were thoroughly satisfied that Eliza Monigail was no other than Cecilia Campbell. The old domestic said, "These are the real marks, and these are the real features; I would know her among a million." Mrs Campbell took Cecilia to her arms, and pressed her to her bosom, exclaiming, "My own, my long-lost Cecilia, I have found you at last!"

Mr Campbell, who had been angling in the lake, just returned after this scene had ended. He was surprised, on entering the parlour, to see his wife's face lighted up with a joyous expression, to which for many years it had been a stranger. "What," said he, "makes you so happy?—have you had letters from Scotland?" "No," said she; "but I wish to introduce you to a young friend of mine," (turning to Cecilia,) "Miss Cecilia Campbell of ——," (naming his own estate,) "from Scotland." He was then informed of the evidence by which the identification had been made complete. Sharper, however, than his wife or her maid, he at once recognised the features of his own daughter, and embraced her with the most enthusiastic joy. The day was one of unmingled happiness. Poor Cecilia was perfectly bewildered in the vortex of passing events, and could hardly realise her position. She by and by proposed returning to Mr Monigail's house. To this her mother strenuously objected, and said she would on no account part with her any more. Mrs Monigail was accordingly sent for, and the discovery fully and satisfactorily explained. While she, on the one hand, expressed herself highly delighted at Eliza's elevation, she was, on the other, overwhelmed with grief at parting with her, being as devotedly attached to her as if she had been her own daughter.

Mrs Monigail next proceeded to explain how Eliza became an inmate in her family. She mentioned that there was an old woman named Sarah M'Cann, who resided about twelve miles distant, who, in company with some others, had for many years traversed the country as a tinker or gipsy, and who had long been in use to supply her and her husband with spoons, articles of tin-ware, and other things in the line of her business as a tinker. She had told the woman, about ten years ago, that, as she (Mrs Monigail) had no family of her own, she would very willingly adopt and educate any nice female child whose parents, from inability to maintain her comfortably themselves, would agree to part with her on condition that she should be maintained and brought up comfortably, and well educated. She told her also that, if any nice child who was an orphan,—without father, or mother, o near relations,—were found, she would willingly engage to adopt and educate her in like manner. She likewise promised Mrs M'Cann to remunerate her for her trouble. But, she said, it never for an instant entered into her (Mrs Monigail's) mind that the woman would steal a child, much less the child of a man of rank. When she brought little Eliza to her, she was so highly pleased at receiving such a beautiful child, that she gave her five pounds for her trouble. She informed Mrs Monigail that the child was an orphan who had lately lost both parents, and been left without any means of support, and that the parish authorities had given her possession of the little girl on the assurance that a lady in Ireland had agreed to take and bring her up in a comfortable way.

Mr Campbell now became determined that Mrs M'Cann should not be allowed to escape unpunished. He sent for a proprietor in the county of Fermanagh, who had been an associate of his at the university, and who was a county magistrate, to assist him. They discovered that an old woman named Stewart, and her daughter, who lived a few miles distant, had been of the party who accompanied Mrs M'Cann at the time that she carried off little Cecilia, and that both saw her do so. Mr Campbell lost no time, after making this discovery, in communicating with the procurator-fiscal of his own county in Scotland, where the theft took place. The result was that a sheriff's warrant from Scotland immediately arrived, and being endorsed by a magistrate of Ireland, the woman M'Cann was apprehended and transmitted to the prison of the county in Scotland where she committed the offence, it being necessary that all cases should be tried at the *locus delicti*, or place where the offence is committed.

A full precognition having been taken by the procurator-fiscal of all the witnesses necessary to prove the case for the Crown, the prisoner was indicted before the High Court of Justiciary for the crime of child-stealing. Having pleaded not guilty, and a jury being impannelled, the old woman Stewart and her daughter, and a man who was also of the party, proved directly the act of theft, which they saw committed, having been all three present on the occasion. Mr and Mrs Monigail proved having received the child from the accused, and having paid her five pounds. Mr and Mrs Campbell, the old waiting-maid, and a number of other servants and friends, proved incontestably the identity of Eliza Monigail with Cecilia Campbell. The evidence was so complete that the jury, without retiring, unhesitatingly returned a verdict of guilty against the prisoner. The presiding judge, after a most severe address to the prisoner on the enormity of her crime, sentenced her to transportation beyond seas for life.

In the course of the investigation, it was discovered that Mr Campbell had committed two mistakes at the outset of his search for his little daughter. One was, that he did not follow the party of tinkers who had taken their passage in the Irish steamer, though informed of the fact by the superintendent of police at Greenock. The other was, giving credence to the story of the band of tinkers whom he overtook there. It turned out that the story was a pure fiction. They actually saw the theft committed, and knew that M'Cann and her associates, who hastened on with so much precipitation, had taken their passage in an Irish steamer, but, in order to deceive and mislead Mr Campbell, had got up the story about their being to attend a market in the east of Scotland. What was remarkable in the case, was the extreme firmness of the one set of tinkers, in opposition to their own interests, in supporting and screening the other set in their nefarious conduct. The tinkers overtaken by Mr Campbell at Greenock were fully assured of a handsome reward had they told the truth about the other party, yet they exerted themselves to support and screen them.

THE INDUSTRIOUS SMUGGLER.

ABOUT forty years ago the laws for the prevention of smuggling were extremely lax and ineffectual. A party detected in the act of distillation usually forfeited the still and the materials employed, with such whisky already manufactured as was found in his custody. Some years later, the laws became much more stringent. The duty on whisky was greatly lowered, while, on the other hand, the penalties imposed for smuggling were made extremely heavy. The result was that, superior whisky being to be had at a comparatively cheap rate, the gains of the smuggler were diminished; and any attempt to smuggle was so hazardous, involving as it did a ruinous penalty, that smuggling became nearly exploded, and almost unknown. Hence the former vigilance of the excise officials became lulled, the existence of whisky-smuggling being considered at an end.

Mr T. E——, a farmer from Ireland, about thirty years ago took a large arable farm on the west coast of Scotland. He was an active, industrious man, a skilful agriculturist, and his farm, though extending to many hundred arable acres, was in a few years placed in first-rate order. The house and farm-steading stood on the brow of a declivity gently sloping towards the south-east. Closely behind the house, and between it and the sea, stood a steep craggy ridge, the side of which, toward the north-west, had a descent towards the sea very steep and rugged. Near the house, and close to the brow of the ridge, was a limekiln, which was observed to be almost always in use, and, owing to its elevated situation, its smoke was seen by all the inhabitants of the adjoining part of the country to a great distance. This caused no surprise, as every one knew that he used much lime, as well as other manures, in following out his system of high farming. He was held up to all his neighbours as a paragon of skill and industry. A number of years passed, till T. E——'s lease was drawing to a close; the smoke from the kiln continued to curl in the air, and the farm and crops to improve in appearance.

Along the side of the ridge next to the sea there ran a stream of considerable size, which, during rain, was usually much swollen, and diminished to a tiny rivulet in dry weather. It slanted along the side of the ridge till it came to nearly opposite the back of E——'s farm-steading, where, turning abruptly at a right angle, it descended straight to the sea, forming a deep gully with a bed of large stones, and its steep banks were densely covered with brushwood and whin-bushes. At the junction of this stream with the sea there was a point of land about a hundred yards in length, projecting into the sea. There being a considerable depth of water on the one side of this point, a quay was formed for the more convenient shipment of Mr E——'s farm produce, as well as for receiving loads of coal, tiles, timber, and other necessaries required by him. The quay being on Mr E——'s ground, it was entirely in his private occupancy; but he sometimes, though seldom, gave permission to some of the neighbouring farmers to use it. A private road, for the exclusive use of his farm, branched off from the public road, passing along the shore and the base of the ridge to the private quay where it terminated. Though E——'s house and farm-steading were thus close to the sea-shore and the quay, the craggy ridge only being between them, yet, from the precipitous nature of the ridge, the shore was wholly inaccessible for either carriages or foot-passengers, except by a circuitous route of two or three miles, which had to be travelled with carts when the farm produce or other effects were to be conveyed to or from the quay.

A year or two before the end of E——'s lease, a cask or two of whisky had been seen at the quay by some fishermen, and which were soon after removed by some party or other unknown; but though it was supposed by the excise officers, to whom the circumstance became known, that E——

or his people could not fail to have seen the casks there, and to be cognisant of the fact of some one having landed them from a boat or vessel, and subsequently removed them, they did not deem it prudent to adopt any measures on the occasion. No other mode of the casks coming there but by sea occurred to the officers; and as they had no information or evidence as to the party who landed them, and no direct evidence against E—— or his servants, they judged it safer to say nothing on the subject, but quietly to watch any suspicious craft that might land similar casks.

No other discovery was made by the excise until a month or two before the close of E——'s lease. About that time some men, who were privately employed by the revenue officers to watch suspicious vessels, discovered in the gully near the quay, concealed among the brushwood, a number of whisky-casks, and on watching to see who would come to remove them, they observed, about three o'clock in the morning, Mr E——'s overseer and two of his servants coming in a stealthy manner, and removing the casks on board a sloop which was moored at the quay, and which had the day before received on board a quantity of Mr E——'s bags with grain. The watchers' authority did not extend to making seizures. They, however, immediately hastened to inform their employers of what they had seen; but before a party arrived to seize the vessel, she had sailed, and was out of sight, and nobody could say in what direction she had proceeded, as she had set sail early in the morning, when the casks were shipped.

Notwithstanding the failure to seize the vessel, evidence was thus obtained that Mr E—— was engaged in smuggling. Accordingly, after the lapse of three weeks in endeavouring, but in vain, to procure evidence as to the place whence the whisky came, and where it was manufactured, it was at length resolved to apprehend Mr E——, and bring him to trial on the grave charge of smuggling, on account of his servants having been seen shipping the casks. The evidence of one man was also obtained who had seen Mr E—— looking on during part of the time when the shipment was taking place. Luckily for him, he received private information of all that was going on, and during these three weeks, accordingly, he was by no means idle. He had for some time back, and before any question of smuggling arose, determined on emigrating to the colonies or the United States at the close of his lease. Now that he was likely to be involved in a smuggling prosecution, he not only was fully confirmed in his previous resolution, but determined that his destination should be the United States of America. He had for a year before been busy disposing of his furniture and effects, except what was required for his immediate use till his departure. In about three weeks after the discovery last referred to, a party of officers with two constables arrived at E——'s house with a warrant for his apprehension. He affected the utmost surprise at any suspicion being entertained against him, and still greater at the authorities considering it necessary to apprehend him, seeing that his position and means were a sufficient guarantee that he would appear to answer any charge, and undergo any trial to which he might be subjected, if they really, after mature deliberation, resolved on such a measure.

The supervisor of excise of the district, who was present, and who was on intimate terms of friendship with E——, informed him that nobody could doubt his respectability and perfect sufficiency to pay any fine that would be imposed, but that the revenue authorities followed certain fixed rules in the case of all parties, whether of rank and wealth or otherwise,—that no distinction was drawn in any case, and that one invariable rule followed was to apprehend every person against whom a prosecution for smuggling was intended. He complained loudly of the inconvenience which he would sustain—that he was engaged shipping a cargo of barley at the quay—that he had a number of letters to answer, and must be allowed time to pack clothes and necessaries to take with him to the town of ——, whither the officers were to convey him. He therefore entreated to be allowed from two to three hours to make his arrangements. He further remarked, that he would prefer to avoid entering the town of —— in broad daylight in custody as a prisoner, and hoped they might convey him thither after it was dark. His requests were considered reasonable, and were at once complied with. The supervisor went to the inn, several miles distant, leaving the officers and constables behind with special instructions—which are always issued on such occasions—to guard the house in case of any attempt at escape, and to bring their prisoner into the town after it became dark.

After the supervisor's departure, an ample supply of food and other refreshments were provided for the officers and constables. Two of them partook of the refreshments at a time, while the other two watched outside, the latter being relieved by the former, and regaled in their turn. At length, two hours and a half having elapsed, the officers knocked at the door, and desired the servant to ask if her master was ready, as it was time to go. She went in, accordingly, and came back saying that he was busy writing a letter, but would be ready in about twenty minutes. Another half hour having passed, the officers once more knocked, and informed the servant that they could not wait longer, and, according to orders, must now go. She affected much surprise, saying she thought she had heard her master coming out to them since they had last knocked. She then went to the room behind, where he had been, but came back saying he was not there, and must have come out. The officers and constables all insisted that he had not, and said that he could not have passed them without their knowledge. They immediately entered the house, and, after calling him loudly by name, and searching every cellar and place about the house where they thought he might be concealed, but all to no purpose, one of the officers hurried off to inform the supervisor of what had happened, the remainder of the party continuing to keep watch at the house, where, they were persuaded, he still remained concealed. The supervisor sent a number of persons who knew Mr E—— by sight in every direction, and through all the neighbouring towns and villages, with the view of tracing him, but to no purpose. They neither saw him themselves, nor any person who had done so, or heard anything of him. A full investigation and precognition, therefore, took place, both with the view of ascertaining where the whisky discovered was manufactured, and of obtaining grounds for a judgment by default against Mr E——. The first thing done immediately after E——'s disappearance, was to employ tradesmen to examine minutely every corner and part of the dwelling-house, to ascertain whether there was no place of concealment where he might be lurking. About the same time, one or two of his servants who still remained—though most of them disappeared at the same time with himself—were fully examined in precognition. Several other persons intimately acquainted with him, and with his affairs, were examined at the same time, when the following facts were fully brought to light:—

The tradesmen employed to examine the house, after a minute investigation in every apartment and closet on the premises, at length came to a press in the parlour where E—— usually sat. On removing the wooden lining of this press, they were surprised to find a door behind it, and, having opened it, they found a dark stair leading down to a subterraneous passage. On procuring lights, and advancing about fifty yards, the passage expanded into a large apartment cut out of the solid rock. It was situated close to the lime-kiln, from which it was ventilated by apertures, and into which a flue passed to convey the smoke from a large fire-place in the apartment. Here they found the traces of where a large still was recently placed and at work, but which had been removed evidently a short time before. Going to one end of this apartment, they found a door leading into another of equal size, which was fitted up as a store for containing many hundred casks; and it appeared to have been recently used; but the casks were all removed. Every step now seemed to throw more light on the proceedings of the fugitive. At the corner of the cask store another door was discovered leading to a sloping passage cut through the rock, with occasional steps of stairs, and occasionally some yards of an inclined plane. At length, after advancing some distance, the investigators heard the noise of a running stream, and, pushing aside one or two large flags, which were placed there to conceal the outlet of the passage, they found themselves on the banks of the deep gully, and about thirty or forty yards from the quay on the sea-shore. Here was most unexpectedly but fully discovered a private place of concealment of the most cunning construction that probably was in existence in the days of Dirk Hatterick. Its discovery threw complete light on the proceedings of E——; and if anything was wanting in its complete development, it was thoroughly supplied by the different parties who underwent precognition.

Mr E—— appeared to have commenced the occupation of smuggling almost from the beginning of his lease. The curling smoke proceeding from his lime-kiln, instead of being produced by the burning of lime, proceeded from the distillery. A little lime was occasionally burned to avert suspicion; but nearly all the large quantities of lime used on the farm were brought from Larne in Ireland, and the vessels which brought it were reloaded with whisky, conveyed by the private passage through the gully to the quay, whence it was conveyed to Ireland, and there privately disposed of. It was ascertained that he had disposed of vast quantities of whisky in this manner, and must, from first to last, have realised prodigious profits. He paid large wages to his servants, who accompanied him in his flight. The nest was now discovered, but the birds were all flown.

E—— had private notice of the excise authorities' intentions about a month before the attempt was made to apprehend him, and he made his preparations with the utmost assiduity and despatch. He collected the amount of every account due to him, and disposed of all his remaining crops, and of his cattle and horses. This excited no suspicion, since it was known he was to remove at the next term of Whitsunday, which was in a couple of months thereafter. He raised all his money from the banks in which it was deposited, and got gold instead of paper money, on the allegation that he was to remove to England. He next packed up all the articles of value and furniture about the house, leaving only such of the latter as was bulky and of least value. Within a day or two of the time when the officers called to apprehend him, he had the whole, including his money, conveyed down the secret passage to the quay, and placed on board a sloop, which was brought there ostensibly to convey a cargo of barley to market. Immediately after the officers called with the warrant, instead of writing letters, as he pretended, he and three or four of his men-servants conveyed the remainder of the articles intended to be shipped, down the private passage, put them on board the sloop, and, embarking themselves, within half an hour or an hour after the officers called with the warrant, took advantage of an east wind, and immediately set sail. A larger vessel was chartered by certain other parties in Ireland, who were to proceed along with him to the United States. They were met, accordingly, by the larger ship on the coast of Ireland. and E——'s effects and himself and servants being taken on board, they set sail with all despatch across the Atlantic, and proceeded to the Far West, where they were soon located far beyond the reach of Scotch excisemen or constables.

THE CANINE THIEF.

SHEEP-STEALING in Scotland has always stood high as an offence in the scale of aggravation, and previous to the statutes limiting the punishment of death, a conviction under this class of thefts uniformly involved the death of the criminal.

About sixty years ago, several of the store farmers in the Ochil Hills missed sheep from their farms. They employed persons to watch all the outlets from those hills to the turnpike road leading along their base from Kinross to Stirling, as well as the road through Strathearn. This precaution, however, proved of no avail, for no thefts were discovered to have taken place by these outlets, yet sheep coninued to be missed from the farms. Having at ength adopted the plan of watching on the hills hemselves where the sheep were grazing, a dis- overy was speedily effected. Two shepherds who vere one night watching the hill of Tillicoultry, bserved, about three o'clock in the morning, a mall parcel of sheep, about thirty in number, col- ected together and moving westward along, or mmediately behind, the ridge forming the summit f the hill. They could not discover any person lriving them, but on approaching nearer they ob- erved a dog driving them along and occasionally noving round about them to keep them together. The watchers were satisfied that the dog was acting under instructions, yet they could not perceive any erson near, though they saw westward to the dis- ance of nearly two miles. In order to discover vhether the dog was really acting under orders, r merely for its own amusement, one of the vatchers, unaccompanied by any dog of his own, vent up to the parcel of sheep, and affected to turn hem in an opposite direction to that in which the log was driving them. This immediately caused the dog to make up to the man who thus interrupted him, and to bark at him as if intending to attack him. This shewed clearly that the dog was acting under orders from his master, which he did not choose should be countermanded by a stranger.

It may be necessary here to explain that shepherds' dogs are of two descriptions. One kind is that which is employed in driving or hunting sheep or cattle, so as to make them move away from the person who hounds or sets on the dog for that purpose, as in the case of sheep or cattle trespassing on any lands, when the owner of the lands hounds a dog on them and sends them back to their own pasture. The other kind of sheep-dogs is what are termed wearing dogs, which, on being directed to do so, collect and bring sheep or cattle, however distant, back to their masters. The latter class are by far the more valuable, and the dog which the watchers now saw removing the sheep was of this class. The two watchers acted with great caution; the object being, according to their master's instructions, to discover the thief or thieves by whom the depredations were committed, more than to take mmediate possession of the sheep. With this view, hey allowed the dog to proceed with his drove, and ollowed him at some distance. It seemed quite lain that the dog's master walked along the route which he intended the sheep should take, and when he dog lost sight of him he kept the track by the cent. The watchers were amazed by the extreme agacity of the dog, as they saw him keep the sheep ogether before him and drive them on for several niles. On reaching the hill of Alva, they noticed n a small eminence, fully three miles ahead of the log, a man making a motion with his arm, and ooking towards the dog. The latter on noticing he signal, accelerated his speed, and drove the sheep efore him at a quicker pace. The watchers, in case hey might be seen by the dog's master, immediately aid themselves down flat among some ferns near vhere they stood, occasionally peeping out from heir cover to see the course that both master and log would take. At length, on finding that they vere sufficiently distant, they rose from their lair nd followed the sheep, taking care to move with ircumspection. The sheep were by this time more than a mile before them, and they lost sight of the dog's master altogether. At length the sheep passed the hill of Demyat driven by the dog, and having begun to descend from the west shoulder of the hill in a southern direction, it became evident that they were about to emerge from the Ochil Hills on the turnpike road, where the roads from Strathearn and Callender unite a little to the east of Dunblane. The master having taken that route, the dog tracked him thither, driving the sheep before him. The route was extremely well selected, for numerous droves of sheep arrive at that point both from Strathearn and from the direction of Callendar, and not a few at the same point by the road from Kinross along the south side of the Ochil Hills. As suspected, the sheep were driven to the point mentioned near Dunblane. On their reaching the Bridge of Allan, a few miles further south, the watchers, who had followed the dog and sheep closely, and were now on the public road a little way behind them, saw the dog's master turn back and go among the sheep, being evidently about to take possession of them and drive them before him.

The watchers thereupon rushed forward and took him into custody, and having got assistance at the Bridge of Allan, where they found a constable, they got the sheep put into a pen, and, with the aid of the constable, conveyed the dog's master to Stirling, where he was brought before the sheriff-substitute on a complaint by the procurator-fiscal charging him with sheep-stealing.

The procurator-fiscal having precognosced the two shepherds as witnesses, the owner of the dog was next judicially examined. His name was James Crichton, and he was well known about Stirling and the neighbourhood as a small drover or dealer in sheep and cattle, who periodically visited that district to purchase sheep and cattle for the southern markets.

The declaration he emitted was as ingenious as the plan he adopted in removing the sheep. He denied most pointedly having anything whatever to do with the removal of sheep from the Ochil Hills. He said that he had occasion to be in Strathearn in the course of his business, and being hurried in order to overtake the Lockerbie market, he took a short cut across the Ochil Hills; that on his way through the hills he lost his dog, which appeared to have fallen behind; and having turned to seek him about the hill of Alva, he saw him with some sheep at the distance of some miles, when he motioned to him with his hand to bring him away from the sheep, and called to him as loud as he could. He said he thought he had left the sheep, and expected that he would soon come up to him; that he (Crichton) at length came to the public road near the Bridge of Allan, where he determined to turn back and search for his dog; that, when returning, he saw the dog on the road with a few sheep, which he went to examine, and intended to leave them at the Bridge of Allan in charge of the innkeeper, to be given to the owner, whoever he might be, when he was taken into custody. This version of his conduct was so plausible that the sheriff, notwithstanding the evidence of the two shepherds, had some difficulty in committing the accused. He, however, did so, and the case was reported, as is usual in important cases, to the Crown lawyers in Edinburgh for instructions. A mmunication was received in a few days from e Crown agent, bearing that the evidence seemed sufficient, and directing that the accused should set at liberty.

Crichton, on being liberated from prison, caused s agent to address a letter to the tenant of Tilliultry farm, threatening an action for reparation, account of his apprehension and imprisonment; d, emboldened by success in his acquittal, he relved again to try his hand on the Ochil flocks. e thought that the owners, intimidated by his reatened action, and despairing of a conviction ter what had taken place, would not trouble emselves further in sending persons to watch the lls. He accordingly renewed his visits. The storeasters of the Ochils, however, so far from relaxg, redoubled their exertions. They ascertained at the sheep were generally missed about the ne of, or immediately before, the Dumfries and ckerbie markets. Before the first Lockerbie arket, therefore, which took place in a few weeks ter Crichton's liberation, they resolved to adopt ery means in their power to procure proper evidence of any theft that might occur. They saw clearly that the two watchers had acted rather precipitately in pouncing upon Crichton at the Bridge of Allan, before he had actually taken possession of the sheep, or driven them some distance before him on the road. They accordingly secured the services of an able detective at Stirling to watch when Crichton came up. They did the same thing at Falkirk and Beattock, taking care at the same time to watch on the hills as formerly, but with still greater privacy. The watchers were clothed in green dresses of the colour of the grass, and caps of the same description, for the purpose of aiding their concealment. Two watchers so clothed, who were concealed among some stunted brushwood on the hill of Menstrie, observed, one morning between two and three o'clock, a parcel of upwards of thirty sheep driven by the identical dog of Crichton which the Tillicoultry shepherds had formerly detected. He was driving the sheep westward, as before. One of the watchers having remained to follow at a distance, and watch the progress of the dog and sheep, the other descended the hill to ɛnstrie village, from whence an express was sent a pony to the detective at Stirling, informing n of what had been discovered. The watcher who nained on the hill followed the sheep to Demiet ll, but did not observe either Crichton or any ıer person in front of the drove. It would seem ıt Crichton had determined to avoid being seen the hill near to the sheep, and, trusting to the g's admirable training and sagacity, he kept a mber of miles ahead, while the dog drove the ɛep before him, and tracked with great precision scent the course that his master took, without viating from it. The dog and sheep, after coming Demiet, went round the shoulder of the hill, and erged on the public road, as formerly, near to junction of the Perth and Callender roads. The tcher, however, who now approached the sheep l dog, could not, as formerly, perceive the dog's ster near the sheep. The dog, however, drove m before him along the road towards Stirling, watcher following at a considerable distance. being now six o'clock in the morning, and it ng impossible to avoid crossing the bridge at

Stirling with the sheep, and passing through the town, it was evident that the dog could hardly drive the sheep alone through the streets of a large town. Accordingly the watcher, who knew Crichton by sight, saw him watching for the dog at the end of the bridge, and on the drove coming up he took possession of it, and proceeded to drive the sheep through the town of Stirling.

The Stirling detective, along with another trusty man whom he employed, had from several points watched the movements of the dog, and sheep, and of Crichton, from the time they left the hills and came upon the public road, and they were quite prepared to procure the evidence required. The person whom the detective employed, was a man engaged to assist the fleshers at the Stirling slaughter-house. He had been a number of years a shepherd at Alva, and knew all the sheep-marks on the different farms in that neighbourhood. He also was an acquaintance of Crichton, whom he had often met at Doune and other markets. The detective got himself dressed in the habit of a small country farmer, or farm-overseer, and by arrange-ıt waited in a small inn at the foot of Broad eet, while the employée was to make up to chton as if by accident, and to bring the detec- ɜ to him as a customer. The employée accord- ly walked along the street, passed the sheep, l noticing Crichton as if by accident, after the al salutations, complimented him on his nice ve, and asked him the news from the north. He ı said, "By the by, there was a man at the ıghter-house about an hour ago, like a country ner, who said something about his wanting a few ep, if he has not left the town perhaps you and might deal. He was at Shaw's Inn; I think he l he came from Campsie. He did not say what l of sheep he wanted, but if you like I will go 'n and get him to come up if he is not gone y." Crichton, delighted at the idea of getting ; of his drove without further trouble, at once roved of the suggestion and promised the other re for his trouble. The latter went off accord- y, and brought the alleged Campsie farmer up where Crichton waited with his drove. The ıer, aided by his assistant the slaughter-house employée, examined the whole stock minutely, the latter noticing carefully the marks all the while, and ascertaining that they belonged to the farms of Alva and Menstrie. The pseudo farmer at length said that what he wanted was gimmers (two year old ewes,) but he observed there were only two in the drove. He said he would have given him an excellent price for the whole drove had they been all gimmers. They therefore parted, the detective as well as his assistant having noted carefully the ear-marks and face-burns of the different sheep.

Crichton now drove the sheep through Stirling, and proceeded along the road towards Falkirk without interruption. He observed, in a park close to the road-side near Falkirk, a man, apparently a country farmer, with his coat off and a spade in his hand, and a younger man in a coarser dress also without his coat, and a pick in his hand. The latter seemed the servant of the former, and they both appeared to be engaged clearing an open drain or sewer close to the road. The farmer, after saluting Crichton in the ordinary way, asked if he was going far south, to which he replied he was going to e Lockerbie market. The farmer asked him if he ould sell any of his drove here, and if he had any e-hogs in the lot. He said he would sell to any rson, but that he had only four hogs, and of these ly two were ewes. He (the farmer) said he wanted score, otherwise he might have dealt with him. e examined the drove, and complimented him on e good quality of the different animals. He took ecial notice of the marks, which he observed were of two kinds. After some other indifferent conrsation, Crichton moved on with his drove. The pposed farmer was no other than the Falkirk tective, and the man supposed to be his servant as his assistant or concurrent. The latter knew ichton well by sight from having often seen him Falkirk and Stirling markets, though Crichton d not recognise him. Crichton little thought how any traps had been laid for him. The same eveng the detective at Stirling arrived in Falkirk, and ined by the one there and his assistant, all three arted at an early hour in the morning, and overking Crichton some miles to the north of Beattock, ok him into custody. The Stirling detective told him that he liked his company so much when he last saw him that he wished to cultivate his further acquaintance, and the Falkirk detective asked him ironically if he had not yet got a score of hogs for him. Nothing could exceed the chagrin and consternation of Crichton when he saw how completely he had been circumvented and entrapped. When he was shewn the warrant of a justice of the peace for apprehending and for conveying him to Dumfries, and the handcuffs were put on him, his bold demeanour entirely forsook him. He was certainly clever and not without quickness of apprehension. His present daring conduct, therefore, after the former proceedings seems inexplicable. Yet it is what often occurs in the history of crime. When a criminal once defeats a prosecution and escapes conviction, he generally becomes bold and daring, and not unfrequently acts so as to place himself in the very grasp of criminal authority. This would seem to be the origin of the apothegm, "*Quem Deus vult perdere prius dementat*"—"Whom God wishes to destroy he first renders mad." One ould certainly suppose that Crichton's sanity of ind had on this occasion wholly forsaken him.

The two detectives from Stirlingshire being joined y him at Beattock, they got the sheep placed in a ark, and conveyed their prisoner to Dumfries, here he was dealt with by the procurator-fiscal ad sheriff, and, after a remand and full precogni-on, taken partly in Stirlingshire and partly in umfriesshire, he was finally examined and com-itted for trial. In Scotland, when a party com-its a theft in one county, and brings the stolen ffects into another, it is optional to have him ommitted and tried either in the county where e effects were originally taken possession of by e accused, or in any other county into which he as brought them. In this case, therefore, the ffects having been brought to Dumfriesshire, it as determined to have the case disposed of there, nd it was set down for trial at the Dumfries ircuit Court of Justiciary.

The case excited great interest throughout the istrict, not more on account of Crichton being famed as a notorious and dexterous sheep-stealer, than the great celebrity of his dog for its sagacity and wonderful exploits. It was an object of much curiosity, and considered one of the wonders of the county. It was known to track its master, and drive sheep after him, when he was five or six miles distant, and had, it was understood, enabled the master to effect many thefts with impunity. Hence crowds came to see so famous an animal. On the indictment being read charging the prisoner with the theft from Alva and Menstrie farms, he pleaded not guilty, and the trial proceeded accordingly. The proof of guilt was clear and decisive. The two watchers proved having seen the dog driving the sheep along the hills from Menstrie, and tracing them to Stirling Bridge. They identified the dog, which they knew as that of the prisoner. They likewise swore to having seen the sheep taken possession of by the prisoner, whom they knew to be Crichton, and now identified at the bar. They also swore to the sheep so taken being part of the stock of Alva and Menstrie farms. The Stirling detective and his concurrent proved the marks of the sheep, and that the prisoner had them in his possession, and was driving them on the streets of Stirling, and had offered them for sale. The concurrent also proved that they were part of the stock of Alva and Menstrie. Similar evidence was given by the detective at Falkirk and his concurrent. Intense interest was excited in a crowded court when the dog was brought in to be identified as the dog that drove the sheep, and as belonging to the prisoner. The case was so clearly established that, after a short address from the advocate-depute, and a short but effective charge from the judge, (the prisoner's counsel declining to say anything,) the jury, without leaving their seats, returned a unanimous verdict of guilty against the prisoner. The prisoner was condemned to be hanged, and was accordingly executed at Dumfries the following month.

The public at large were satisfied that Crichton had met with his just deserts; but immediately after the execution an act was perpetrated by some inferior parties connected with the prison or burgh that created general indignation. The poor dog, so faithful to his master's behests, was hanged in the court of the prison, as if the poor, dumb animal could know to whom the sheep belonged, which, from fidelity to his master, he removed from their owners. Had the occurrence taken place some years later, the parties engaged in this reckless piece of cruelty might have been smartly punished under Mr Martin's Act.*

* The above narrative is substantially true. The thefts, trial, and execution took place about sixty years ago, and Crichton was the real name of the convict who was executed at Dumfries, as stated. The exploits of the dog excited great curiosity; and the poor animal was barbarously destroyed, as mentioned.

THE PIRATE.

BETWEEN thirty and forty years ago, the merchant ship *Hecla* of London sailed from Quebec for the Thames. She was ship-rigged, of 800 tons burden, a substantial and commodious craft with great breadth of beam, in which ample capacity was more studied in the construction than velocity in sailing, and she was better adapted for stowing a large cargo, and comfortably accommodating passengers than making quick voyages. A considerable part of her was occupied with a cargo of flour, grain, and hides, and the remainder was engaged by the government to convey between thirty and forty soldiers of the —— regiment of infantry, in charge of a lieutenant, with a dozen of artillerymen, being a remnant whom a transport lately dispatched to England could not accommodate, and also a quantity of government stores. There were twelve cabin passengers, and a crew of about thirty seamen. The weather was fine, and being at a season when the St Lawrence with its wooded banks and islands was peculiarly attractive, they weighed anchor in high spirits, and glided down the river with a gentle breeze, as if moving through fairy-land. At length they entered the Gulf of St Lawrence, exhibiting an expanse of water second only to the ocean in extent. Here a dead calm retarded their progress for some days. This afforded the opportunity to four of the cabin passengers, who were determined sportsmen and dexterous hands at the fowling-piece and rifle, to amuse themselves and greatly improve the supplies of the ship's larder. Having first employed some time in an open boat, large quantities of wild duck, widgeon, wild geese, and other aquatic fowls were bagged. They next landed on the shores and one or two islands, where they killed a number of deer, racoons, wild turkeys, and partridges. By the time the breeze sprung up, at the end of three days, the ship's larder was filled to overflowing with game sufficient to supply the table of the first cabin during the whole voyage.

A breeze having at length sprung up from the north-west, the *Hecla* got under way and commenced to beat down the gulf, making considerable progress, though the wind was not fair. In a few days they passed the island of Anticosti on their left, and bade adieu to the Canadian shores. The ssme steady breeze continuing, nothing new occurred for nearly a week. They passed between Newfoundland and Cape Breton, and were at length fairly ushered into the broad Atlantic, steering a point or two to the south to catch the gulf stream. When about a hundred and fifty miles to the west of Cape Breton, the captain and some of the cabin passengers were amusing themselves on the quarter-deck looking through a powerful Dolland spy-glass belonging to the ship. They noticed a far way off a small speck on the southern horizon, which appeared to be increasing in size, and which the captain's experienced eye soon discovered to be a sail. On its approaching a few miles nearer, the captain, on again looking towards it, became extremely suspicious of its character from its movements. It did not seem to be steering for Europe, nor yet for the American coast, but to be pointing directly towards his ship, or at right angles to its course. He further observed that it was of a sharp build, fitted to sail with speed, and having crowded sails was making great way. The master therefore did not lose a moment in holding a council with his two mates, also with the lieutenant in command of the infantry soldiers, and the sergeant of artillery in charge of the artillerymen. Two of the most intelligent of the cabin passengers were likewise requested to attend. The master, who was a man of great experience and energy, informed them of what he saw, and strongly suspected in regard to the approaching sail. He said from her build, rig, and general appearance, and above all from the course in which she was sailing—right upon the *Hecla*—he could not doubt that she intended mischief. He therefore suggested, that for their own safety as well as that of the vessel and cargo, they should use their utmost exertions to aid him in repelling the attack which he had no doubt would be made. He said his ship had only one swivel—a nine-pounder, on the forecastle, but he observed that part of the government stores included two pieces of ordnance—a twenty-four and a twelve-pounder, which were stowed on deck. He suggested that these should be immediately placed in a proper position on deck, and if there was powder and shot among the government stores on board, that they should be immediately got up on deck, and the two guns charged. The sergeant told him there was an ample supply of powder and shot on board, both grape and round shot, and that he would immediately get the two guns placed in position near the centre of the ship, one on each side of the mainmast. The artillerymen were therefore immediately set to work, and in a very short time the guns were placed in position and fully charged, as was also the swivel. The captain next addressed himself to the lieutenant in command of the infantry, suggesting that his men should have their muskets all loaded and ready to fire on the crew of the pirate at the proper time.

The lieutenant heartily assented, and said that besides their own muskets which each soldier had in his custody, there were 100 stand of muskets in the government stores on board, and a large supply of ball cartridge. He would therefore, he mentioned, give each of his men, in addition to his own musket, another one from the store, so that each could fire off two muskets. He would thereafter have about sixty muskets still remaining in the store, which could, with a corresponding supply of ball cartridges, be distributed among such of the crew and passengers as were able to use them. This was speedily accomplished. The muskets and cartridges were unpacked and got on deck, and the soldiers supplied each with an additional musket and twelve rounds of ball cartridge. The remainder of the muskets were given to the cabin passengers and about two-thirds of the crew, the remaining third being in charge of the ship and sails. The four sportsmen who had so effectually stocked the larder, preferred their own rifles and fowling pieces, but were amply supplied with powder. In this way there were thirty-seven soldiers, twenty seamen, and twelve passengers supplied each with two loaded muskets and twelve rounds of ball cartridge, and of large guns there were in charge of the artillerymen, a twenty-four, a twelve, and a nine-pounder cannon, fully loaded with grape-shot. Everything was therefore prepared to give the pirates a warm reception.

At the outset of these preparations, the captain adopted the judicious plan of concealing as much as possible from the pirates his condition of defence, and of inducing them to believe that there was no ordnance, and very few small-arms, on board the *Hecla*. With this view, he erected an awning amidships, where the artillerymen were placing the two large guns, so as completely to conceal both guns and men. The swivel was in like manner concealed by some bales of goods being placed near it, and a tarpaulin thrown over the whole. It was next suggested by the captain that the soldiers should all doff their coats, so as to conceal their military uniforms, which injunction was carefully attended to, a circumstance which created no inconvenience, from the fineness of the weather. The captain made another important suggestion, which the parties consulted also agreed to adopt. This was, that a party should be assembled on board the *Hecla*, as if for the purpose of boarding the pirate, and that they should deport themselves in such a way as to induce the belief on the part of the piratical crew that boarding was their intention, and that they should go through the process of lowering one of the boats, as if to be used for the purpose. Where a crew is numerous, but without ordnance or other fire-arms, or slenderly provided with them, it is the usual, and often the only possible resource, to board the vessel of their opponent. To present the appearance of being about to follow this course was, therefore, part of the captain's scheme, to induce the belief that they were wholly helpless as regarded fire-arms. Some dozens of the crew and passengers were accordingly stationed on the larboard side of the ship. They were provided, some with cutlasses, others with swords, a few with carving-knives and miscellaneous weapons. These arrangements being completed, the master gave orders to direct the vessel's course due north instead of east, so as to give the *Hecla* the appearance of attempting to make her escape from the pirate, and thereby affording another indication that the former was without the means of defence.

These arrangements being all completed, the pirate, which made nearly double the way of the *Hecla*, was now only about three miles distant. She was barque-rigged, apparently about four hundred tons burden, and seemed to have a numerous crew for her size—numbering, probably, between forty and fifty men. She had now hoisted the flag of the Chilian Republic,—the unmistakeable ensign of nearly all the pirates in those seas. She was gaining fast on the *Hecla*, and in three-quarters of an hour more, being only about a furlong distaut, she hailed her, demanding "From whence and whither bound?" The master replied, "From Quebec, for London;" and in the same breath asked, "Whence are you, and whither bound?" "From Valparaiso," replied the pirate, "and bound for hell;" and added, "What cargo have you got?" "Why do you ask?" said the master of the *Hecla*; "do you wish to buy provisions?" "No," said the pirate; "but you must surrender your ship and cargo, or I 'll blow you to pieces." "No, I won't," said the captain of the *Hecla*, in the most defiant tone; "we will die first." This was followed by a shot of grape from one of the pirate's guns, which damaged part of the companion of the *Hecla*, and slightly wounded one of the seamen on the left shoulder. This was the time for the pseudo boarding party to show themselves; and accordingly, on a concerted signal they immediately assembled on a conspicuous part of the forecastle, flourishing their cutlasses, swords, knives, &c., and another party at the same time lowered and launched one of the *Hecla's* boats. The pirates at once came to the conclusion that the *Hecla* had no guns, though a very numerous crew, and that they were determined, as a *derniere ressource*, if possible to board and take the pirate by dint of numbers. The pirates, therefore, did not fire any more guns at present; but the gun which was discharged was immediately reloaded, and it and other two guns,—all they were possessed of, and which appeared not to exceed the calibre of nine-pounders,—were kept pointed to the water, waiting till the boarding-boat of the *Hecla* should come alongside the barque, when, by taking a proper aim, they felt confident of sinking her. The whole hands on board the pirate were likewise assembled in a dense cluster about the waist of the vessel, on the larboard side, and all provided with boarding-pikes, thinking doubtless that the boarding would for certain be attempted there; and, in case the guns should fail to sink the boat, that they would next repel the boarding. While the whole hands on board the pirate were thus employed, clustered in one dense mass, watching till the boat would come round either end of the *Hecla* to attack them,—both ships being only about twenty yards apart,—the awning and other obstructions on the deck of the *Hecla* were removed, and instantly the three heavy guns, with a well-directed aim by the artillery-gunners, poured a broadside on the devoted crowd of pirates who, one would suppose, had massed themselves on one spot to be exposed to wholesale destruction. Simultaneously with the fire of the heavy guns, there were poured into them with deadly effect seventy shots from muskets, to which were instantly added seventy other shots from the additional musket supplied to each man. At so unexpected and fatal an attack from the *Hecla,* the pirates uttered loud yells of terror and despair, and in a few seconds, on the smoke clearing away, an appalling scene presented itself. The three heavy guns, which were loaded almost to the muzzle with grape-shot, and aimed with perfect precision, actually ploughed three broad avenues through the crowd of unfortunate pirates placed so near them, and in so exposed a situation. The twenty-four-pounder was placed right opposite to the pirate's mainmast, and after dealing destruction to a number of the hands crowded near the mast, the shot hit the mast and broke it about two feet from the deck. It fell over, accordingly, in a half-broken state, with its yards and sails, to the one side of the ship, destroying the ship's trimming, and impeding her sailing. The crew of the pirate were forty-six in number. Of these, eighteen were shot dead by the first broadside of the *Hecla,* and as many more severely wounded, ten of them mortally, so that only ten hands remained to work the ship. They therefore thought of nothing now but how to make their escape. The carpenter, though wounded, and another survivor, were attempting with hatchets to cut away the mainmast, when a ball from the rifle of one of the four sportsmen on board the *Hecla* shot the carpenter dead. Another hand having taken up the carpenter's hatchet, at length managed, with the assistance of the other man, to cut away the mainmast; but by the time it was partially got overboard, both men were severely wounded by musket-shots from the *Hecla*. Another hand who took the wheel, and several who ascended the shrouds to adjust the sails, were all hit and severely wounded.

The *Hecla* had now got all her guns reloaded, and was prepared to give as effective a broadside as the first; but after fully reconnoitering the condition of the pirate, and observing that the crew were in a state next to annihilation, the captain called on them instantly to surrender, or that he would sink the barque. The surviving pirates, however, knew the alternatives proposed was offering a mere choice of deaths. They were aware that, if captured and carried to England, they would be hanged as pirates; while, should they fail to make their escape from the *Hecla,* they would be shot or sunk; and, on the other hand, if by any chance they could make their escape, they would be saved. They therefore firmly resolved to turn their back to the wind's eye, and, with what sails they could still command, if possible make their escape. They therefore gave a decided refusal to the summons to surrender. Observing that the man at the wheel was constantly selected for the shots from the small-arms of the *Hecla,* they piled bales of goods and other articles round the wheel for his protection. They also got four of the most active of the survivors to run up the ratlines with the utmost speed to adjust the sails. But by the time this was only partially effected, all four were hit and compelled to descend, one of them falling mortally wounded before he reached the deck. In their present condition, therefore, the pirates found that their speed of sailing was hardly equal to that of the *Hecla.* The master of the latter now formed the resolution of boarding the enemy's barque in reality, which he thought their crippled state would enable him to effect without much danger. He accordingly got a boat launched, and manned with three dozen of picked men from the soldiers, artillerymen, and crew, and from a few volunteers of the cabin-passengers. Each of these was armed with a cutlass or sword, a pistol, and a revolver. The boat, which was in command of the first mate, was directed to remain close at the stern of the *Hecla* until a broadside of the large and small guns should be given to the pirate, and immediately thereafter to make for the larboard of the pirate's waist, and effect a boarding before the confusion consequent on the broadside should terminate. A broadside was now given with even more effect than formerly, the vessels being nearer to each other. The boarding party immediately made for the larboard side of the barque, as arranged, and, after a feeble resistance, and the exchange of a few pistol-shots, inflicting one or two slight wounds, succeeded in boarding the barque, and, overpowering the seven or eight who, alone of the whole crew, remained effective, they disarmed and bound them. On examining the pirate's decks, a fearful sight presented itself. To the eighteen who were killed outright by the first broadside, eight more were since added who died of their wounds, or were killed by the fire of the *Hecla,* and the whole still lay on deck, as they had originally fallen, in pools of blood and gore. Ten or a dozen lay on deck badly wounded, and many of them in a dying state. Among the dead was the captain, who had been mortally wounded by the first broadside, and had since died. The first mate also lay dead. The second mate survived, and was one of the prisoners. The second broadside completely annihilated the mizzenmast, which went by the board; and the pirate, which a few hours ago was a well-rigged, tidy craft, now lay a dismantled hulk, with only the foremast remaining. The dead bodies being consigned to the deep, and the wounds of the survivors being dressed, and their wants attended to, the prisoners were transferred to the *Hecla.* A jurymast was fitted up in the pirate, which, with the foremast, carried sufficient sail to bring her to England. Ten of the crew of the *Hecla* were placed on board the pirate to navigate her, and both vessels sailed to England in company.

A large amount of gold and silver specie was found on board the pirate; also a prodigious quantity of silver-plate of every description,—doubtless the plunder of many vessels, as well as of houses on shore.

On reaching England, judicial proceedings were instituted against the pirates. The vessel was condemned as piratical, and the surviving pirates being brought to trial, were found guilty of piracy on the high seas, and condemned to death. Four were executed, but after due inquiry into antecedents, the sentence of the remainder was commuted to banishment for life.

It is impossible not to admire the great ingenuity and wonderful tack of the captain of the *Hecla*, in so completely outwitting the pirates, whereby a most formidable, well-armed, and dangerous enemy was not only placed entirely in his power, but the lives of his own men and all bloodshed on their part, as well as his ship, completely saved.

THE RING AND CAP.

A GREAT proportion of burglaries have been traced to the perpetrators by means of some relic left incautiously behind them, or some foot-prints or other signs forming links in the chain of circumstantial evidence.

Early one morning notice was sent to a police station in Liverpool that the premises of Messrs H—— & Co., an American house in —— Street, had been broken into, and that some merchandise and a considerable sum of money had been stolen. Inspector D——, an able and sharp detective, was instantly on the spot. The articles stolen were a box of dollars of the value of £200, twenty pounds weight of cigars, and money in bank-notes and gold to the amount of £220. An entrance had been effected to H—— & Co.'s premises from the floor immediately above them, which had been formerly occupied as a warehouse by another company, but was then empty. The burglars cut a hole through the floor and descended by a rope. Inspector D—— first examined narrowly the floor above, where were several footmarks, and which, though somewhat indistinct, were sufficient to shew that the footmarks were of different lengths, and therefore, that at least two persons were engaged in the operations. The money was taken from a small desk which they had forced open, but it would seem that they must have been scared by some noise, and, in the fear of being discovered, had made a sudden retreat. They left nearly the half of the money in the desk without removing it. They also took only one box of dollars, though another stood beside it which they must have observed and might have taken at the same time. Other signs of a hurried retreat were, that a ring and a foraging cap were dropped on the floor. The ring was probably taken off his finger by one of the parties when in the act of hoisting himself up by the rope to the floor above, when taking their departure from the premises. The foraging cap must have been dropped at the same time. Every part of the cap was examined, outside and in, but no name or initials were found on it. It was, however, somewhat peculiar. It was of a bright green colour, though parts of it were much faded. An unusually large button on the top was of a blue colour, and the ribbons for fastening under the chin were of a bright purple. The leather shade in front of it was square and unusually peaked at the corners. In forcing the desk from which the money was abstracted, the burglars seem to have, in the first place, tried to gain admission by cutting the wood near the lock, and in doing so left about a quarter of an inch of the point of a knife in the wood. This piece of the knife was taken possession of by Mr D——, and wrapped up along with the ring and foraging cap, but no other memorial of the thieves could be found on the premises. On examining the ring it proved to be a diamond ring of great value. There were heads of an antique style carved on either side of the hoop, and inside were the initials F. S. W.

The first essay to discover the culprits was made by means of the foraging cap. It was thought that some of the police force might recognise the cap on account of its colour, and be able to identify the owner. Two of them accordingly, whose beats were near the docks, recognised the cap as worn by a man whom they had seen several times issuing from a lane near the docks. He was usually in the garb of a seaman, and smartly dressed with new clothes. One of them had also seen him with different clothes from that of a seaman, but though they remembered his general appearance, both of them had doubts if they could be certain of recognising him without the green cap. They were directed to keep a look-out, however, but on no account to arrest him or make up to him unless they were sure of their man, and even then they were enjoined to follow him at a distance and ascertain where he resided. One of them saw a man, whom he took to be he that was sought for, enter a river steamer one day, but neither of them could thereafter see him or any one like him.

After the lapse of ten days, inspector D——, as his next course,. fell upon the plan of advertising for the owner of the ring. He represented it as found on the street, selecting a street between that in which Messrs H—— & Co.'s place of business was situated and the docks, so as to lead the owner to suppose that he must have dropped it on his way home after getting out of H—— & Co.'s premises. The advertisement ran thus:—"Found in ——Street a valuable diamond ring with certain initial letters thereon. It will be restored to the owner on his calling at the shop of —— & Co., Lord Street, to-morrow or next day between twelve and one o'clock, identifying the same, and paying the charge for advertising and other expenses."

Next day at the appointed hour Inspector D—— was at the shop mentioned, wearing a moustache and other disguises, and habited as a smartly-dressed shopman. In a short time a dashingly-dressed lady called and asked for the ring, which she said was hers, and she gave the true initials (F. S. W.) and otherwise described it accurately. Mr D—— at once recognised her as Jess Holway, a lady of the town, though she did not recognise him. He said to her, "Oh, I'm sorry I left the ring at home, or you might have got it, but if you leave the address I can send it to-morrow. But," said he, "it is a gentleman's ring, surely *you* don't wear it,—perhaps it belongs to your husband. If so, I should like to deliver it into his own hands, as it is very valuable." She replied, "Oh yes, it belongs to my husband. He's from home to-day, but will return late this evening or to-morrow morning." "You can just leave the address then," replied Mr D——, "and to save your calling again I will send the ring to-morrow by one of the lads, who will get your husband's receipt for its delivery. There will be a few shillings to pay for advertising and a trifle for porterage, which can be paid at the same time." She then gave the address of her husband, "Mr William Hood, No. 41 —— Lane." Mr D—— then said in an indifferent manner, as if the remark had been accidental, "Oh yes, I think I have seen you pass down this street in company with a gentleman who was probably your husband; I think he wore a green foraging cap." "Oh no," said the lady, "that was not my husband, that was Jack Taylor, an intimate friend of his, who generally resides with us. He lives with us at present, but is gone with my husband to the country, and will return along with him." Mr D—— had thus acquired some most important information. He had not only got the name of the owner of the ring, but that of the owner of the cap, and had also got the address of both. He was therefore determined to lose no time in following up the advantage he had obtained.

Having doffed his assumed disguise, Mr D—— dressed himself in a plain suit and went direct to —— Lane, in which resided Jess Holway and her pseudo husband Bill Hood, and their friend Jack Taylor. He called upon a tavern-keeper whom he knew, and on whom he could depend, who lived nearly opposite the residence of the above parties. The tavern-keeper knew well both Hood and Taylor, who were frequently in his house. He said that the girl Holway and Hood lived together as man and wife, though all the neighbourhood knew her to be a street-walker, and in Hood's absence she cohabited with Taylor. It is a remarkable circumstance in the history of crime that a majority of the most determined thieves and burglars have female companions whom they keep and support, but who at the same time cohabit with other men according as it suits the convenience of their purse or their fancy. The tavern-keeper said that both Hood and Taylor bore a bad character, and were often suspected of nefarious proceedings. He identified the ring at once as Hood's, having often seen it on his finger, and having been permitted by him to examine it, and he knew the engraved letters on the inside. He recognised the green cap as Taylor's, and knew it at once when he saw it. These facts were so important that D—— resolved next day to apprehend Hood and Taylor and to search their premises for the stolen property.

Next afternoon the constable, within whose beat —— Lane was situated, sent a message to D—— informing him that Hood and Taylor had returned home. D——, who was waiting the message, was at once in attendance with two active officers. They found the two men sought for over a bottle of wine. On stating the object of the visit, both seemed greatly disconcerted and alarmed, not having the slightest idea that their proceedings were known or suspected by anybody. They in words stoutly denied all knowledge of the robbery, while their manner and alarmed looks wholly betrayed them. On their being informed that their premises were to be searched they shewed the greatest reluctance to permit it, saying that there was no authority for such a proceeding, and that the officers had no right to turn over their property in such a manner. D—— said his instructions were peremptory on the subject. The search therefore proceeded, a police officer being left to watch at the door in case of an exit. On entering the dressing-room of the lady' the *soi disant* Mrs Hood, they found a vast profusion of valuable trinkets and ornaments of dress of every description. These, however, being apparently in use, and there being no evidence that they were stolen, were left untouched. On entering Hood's bedroom, there was found in a press a number of implements used for housebreaking, embracing crowbars of different sizes, screw-drivers, pincers, skeleton keys, implements for picking locks, &c. Among the same articles was found a knife with the point broken off. On afterwards trying it with the fragment of a knife-point found in the desk from which the money was abstracted in the premises of H—— & Co., the two were found to fit exactly, thereby proving that the knife found in the press was the same that was employed in opening the desk in question. In searching the rest of the house there was found in the secret drawer of a portable desk, which was not at first noticed on opening it, the bank-notes and part of the gold stolen from the premises of H—— & Co. The notes all remained, but part of the gold seemed to have been used or spent. Two of the notes which were twenty pound ones were fully identified, H—— & Co. having had a note of the numbers, which they gave to the police. After a lengthened search, which was just about to be abandoned without any further discovery, there was found sunk in the bottom of the water-cistern by which the house was supplied with water, the box of dollars taken from H—— & Co.'s premises. In an unoccupied dark closet, beneath a number of empty boxes, was found a large box filled with valuable silver-plate, most of it of antique patterns, and with family arms and crests engraved thereon. These were evidently the produce of thefts very recently made from private houses. Having secured and sent away the different articles which they found, the officers next conveyed Hood and Taylor themselves to the police-office, and they were brought up for examination before the sitting magistrate next morning.

The testimony against the two prisoners before the magistrate was so strong as utterly to amaze the accused themselves. The proof of the ownership of the diamond ring and the foraging cap, and also the identification of the knife used to cut the desk, by means of the broken fragment, were achievements to them almost incomprehensible. They were advised by their counsel to make no statement before the magistrate, and so they reserved their statements till their trial.

At their trial, they stood charged not only with the burglary and theft from the premises of Messrs H—— & Co., but also with the theft of a number of pieces of valuable plate, part of what was found in the box in Hood's house, important evidence having been discovered as to it from parties from whose houses it was taken. Inspector D—— and the two officers proved having found the diamond ring, foraging cap, and portion of the broken knife, in H—— & Co.'s premises. The ownership of the ring and cap was fully proved by the tavern-keeper and several others, and the finding the knife, from which the fragment was broken, in Hood's bedroom, was proved by Inspector D—— and several officers. The same parties proved finding, also in Hood's residence, the box of dollars and the bank-notes. The ownership of the box and part of the notes was proved by the partners of H—— & Co. The theft of a portion of the silver-plate from the different houses was fully proved, a number of witnesses examined having seen the prisoners lurking at night near the houses from which the plate was taken.

The judge's charge was decidedly unfavourable to the prisoners; and the jury, after a short consultation, unanimously found them guilty of all the charges. They were sentenced to transportation for fourteen years.

THE WHOLESALE FORGER.

THE land-rights of Scotland have long held a high place in public estimation, on account of the thorough security which is afforded both to purchasers and to lenders of money, by means of the records of sasines. Yet experience has shewn that the security even of that system may be to some extent invaded by the devices of a fraudulent impostor.

Mr L——, an old man who held a small farm in a remote part of Roxburghshire, happened to receive from a relative, who died abroad, a legacy of £2000. Mr W. C——, a law practitioner in a town in Lanarkshire, who was acquainted with the legatee, and had heard of his good fortune, threw himself in his way, and the subject of the legacy being referred to, he offered his services in procuring a good investment for the money. He mentioned at the same time that a client of his, a proprietor in Lanarkshire, required a loan of £2000, and that if he chose he would apply to him to take the money in loan, giving in return the security of his estate, which, he said, was ample for the sum in question. He also promised to procure and send him the rental and all other particulars of the estate.

On returning home, Mr C—— sent the farmer a description of the lands, with the names of the several farms on the estate, and a statement of the yearly rent of each, the aggregate amount of which was £785 sterling. The farmer expressed himself highly satisfied, and directed his new agent immediately to get the bond prepared, infeftment passed, and the instrument of sasine recorded. Mr C—— wrote him in reply that his instructions would immediately be complied with, and the bond and sasine sent him as soon as the latter was recorded. The farmer immediately sent him the bank-deposit receipt held by him for the £2000. In the course of a few weeks he received in a packet a bond and disposition in security, subscribed by the person to whom the money was to be lent, the instrument of sasine following thereon, authenticated by Mr C—— himself as the notary who passed the infeftment, and bearing the certificate by the keeper of the register, as duly recorded. Mr L—— placed the bond and sasine in his strong box, thinking himself as secure as if his money had been deposited in the Bank of England. Several years passed. Mr L—— received the interest of his money half-yearly with the utmost punctuality, and thought himself the luckiest of men.

Mr C—— owned a small property near the town where his business was carried on, which gave him a good position in society. He was known to have considerable transactions in railways and other joint-stock undertakings; and although these do not always improve the fortunes of parties engaged in them, yet, from C——'s own account of his speculations, they were highly successful, and had largely increased his fortune. While his speculations proceeded, he frequently discounted bills at different banking-houses, a circumstance which caused no surprise, as his joint-stock transactions, as well as his professional business ones, were extensive and numerous, and the bills so presented were in use to be regularly retired when due. On one occasion he presented a bill for £200 to Mr M——, a private bill-discounter in Glasgow. It bore to be drawn by a party in Ayrshire on, and accepted by, two highly respectable men, one of them a member of Parliament, in their capacity of trustees for a deceased proprietor under his trust-settlement. The bill bore to be blank indorsed by the drawer to Mr C——, who discounted it with the private discounter referred to, and received the money. The discounter's own law-agent happened to call for him on other business just as the transaction was closed, and after C——'s departure Mr M—— mentioned casually to the former the bill transaction, and, having the bill still in his hand, he shewed it to him, remarking that the names were substantial ones. His agent said there surely must be some mistake; for he was pretty certain that the trust mentioned was finally wound-up nearly two years before. The discounter said that could not be, and that C—— himself was a respectable man, and a landed proprietor. On further reflection, however, the discounter judged it as well, as the member of parliament referred to had an agent in Glasgow, and as it could do no harm, to inquire as to the trust being terminated. He accordingly waited on the agent, and was told that the trust was certainly terminated, and wound-up more than eighteen months previously; and he did not think there could possibly be any new bill transactions. Mr M—— triumphantly produced the bill, which he brought with him, and said, (exhibiting it,) "Seeing is believing." The agent, on examining it, said at once that neither of the two signatures were those of the trustees, but, on the contrary, decided forgeries, and very clumsy imitations of those which they were intended to represent. Mr M—— felt confident that Mr C—— himself must have been imposed upon by the drawer of the bill. The agent of the supposed acceptors told him he was acquainted with the drawer of the bill, and knew him to be a highly respectable and substantial man; but as he did not know his signature, he recommended that he should be at once written to, and if he disclaimed the signature, then the whole of the imposture must rest with Mr C——. Mr M—— wrote, accordingly, stating that he held a bill, of which he was drawer, for £200, indorsed by him to Mr C——, of which Messrs (naming the two trustees referred to) were the acceptors; that an acquaintance of his had informed him that the trust in question had been wound-up, and begging to know from him as drawer of the bill, the history of the transaction. Mr M—— received the following letter in reply by return of post:—

"Sir,—I have this moment received your letter of yesterday's date with the most unqualified surprise. I never had any bill transaction with the trustees to whom you refer in my life, and never drew or subscribed any bill to which they were parties; neither did I ever endorse any bill to Mr C——, and never had any money or other business transaction with him in all my life. There must be some singular mistake in the names of the parties, or else a most gross piece of fraud and forgery, as to which you should institute immediate inquiries.—I am, sir," &c.

This seemed a regular poser, and Mr M—— felt truly *nonplussed*. He had ascertained that the names of the two acceptors were forgeries, and not only was the drawer's name also forged, but that gentleman had declared by his letter that he never had any transaction with Mr C—— in his life. What, therefore, was he to do. Matters looked as bad as they could be, but he thought the most prudent course was to write a note to Mr C——, desiring to see him immediately with reference to an important matter connected with the bill which he had discounted a few days previously, without entering into any of the particulars which had come to his knowledge. He wrote him a note to that effect accordingly, but after waiting several days no response came back. He next called at his place of business, but was informed by the clerk that he had gone from home in the morning of the preceding day, and was not to return for some days. He ascertained at the same time that his note requesting an interview had been received the night before he left home. All this in Mr M——'s opinion augured most unfavourably. The residence of the latter was not far distant from that of Mr C——. The note specified that he wished to see him immediately on a matter of importance connected with the bill, yet neither was the request complied with, nor any instructions left with his clerk on the subject. So after waiting three days more, and finding that Mr C—— had not returned home, he thought it right to place the bill and a statement of the whole information he had received regarding it, in the hands of his law-agent, a man of great experience and professional skill.

In a few days Mr M—— received a letter from his agent containing the most alarming revelations. In the first place it was ascertained that Mr C—— had on the morning of his departure gone in great haste to the two banks where he kept his money and drew out from both almost the whole amount at his credit. He also took the greater part of it in gold, alleging that he had been called to England on railway business of great importance and urgency. On the other hand his sister and two nieces who resided in family with him knew nothing of his movements, or at least they said they did not. In the next place, it was found that besides the £200 bill there were other three bills in different banks, and it was ascertained that the whole names in two of these were forgeries. The last but not the least alarming circumstance stated by the agent was, that all these bills and the signatures attached to them, including the £200 bill, were ascertained on minute examination to be wholly in the handwriting of Mr C——, although evidently much disguised.

Every succeeding day revealed new circumstances connected with C——'s affairs. It was ascertained that he took his passage from Greenock on board a Liverpool steamer, that his luggage consisted of two large trunks, several large portmanteaus, travelling bags and boxes. It was discovered through the servants that he had packed up all his trinkets and jewels, and some of the most valuable portions of his silver-plate.

Mr M—— and several other creditors now proceeded without delicacy to take measures against C——'s estate for their security, by executing arrestments of any money and effects they could find in the hands of other parties, and executing inhibitions against his heritable estate. The banking companies who had discounted and held the forged bills, gave information to the procurator-fiscal, by whom a Justiciary warrant was obtained and despatched to Liverpool for the forger's apprehension. It was found on applying to a shipping company, one of whose vessels had sailed from the port of Liverpool for the United States the day before, that a gentleman answering precisely to the description of Mr C—— had sailed on board of the ship under the name of Webster, and, after considerable trouble and inquiry, a gentleman from Glasgow was found who knew Mr C—— by sight, and had been on the quay the day before and seen him go on board, busily superintending the shipment of a number of trunks, portmanteaus, boxes, and other luggage.

It was accordingly arranged to obtain a Secretary of State's warrant for transmission to New York to apprehend and bring him back. Such a warrant was procured and immediately transmitted accordingly.

After the lapse of three or four weeks, intelligence was received that the vessel in which the *soi disant* Webster had sailed was overtaken by a storm, had sprung a leak, and was lost. About two-thirds of the passengers and crew were saved, some of them by taking to the boats, and some by clinging to planks and pieces of floating timber. The remaining third were drowned. Those saved were picked up by a trading vessel bound for Bristol, at which port they were landed a few weeks after being picked up. Soon after being landed at Bristol, a number of the passengers were seated together in a coffee-house, when a person entered the apartment, who evidently had heard of their disaster and the name of the ship, and inquired casually if any of them knew a passenger on board of the name of Webster. A gentleman of the party answered with great promptitute that he did know such a gentleman, but that he was among the drowned. He said he had gone below to attempt to save some property, and on his coming on deck both the long-boat and jolly-boat were filled, and he could not get iuto either; that he again saw him attempting to get at a piece of floating timber, but not being able to swim he could not reach it, and he saw him sinking. This statement immediately got wind, and notices appeared in the Bristol papers, which were copied into all the newspapers in the kingdom, that C——, the noted forger who had sailed for America on board the ship *Enterprise*, was drowned along with a portion of the passengers and crew when that ship sunk. His fate being thus stated with the utmost confidence, the Government and the public prosecutor took no further trouble in regard to his apprehension.

Mr L——, the old Roxburghshire farmer, was seldom or never from home, and had no intercourse with Lanarkshire beyond receiving half-yearly a letter remitting the interest of his bond. He was therefore a long time in learning that C—— had taken French leave of his friends, and embarked for the western hemisphere.. He first heard of it from a friend who had seen it announced in a Glasgow newspaper, but he paid little attention to the circumstance, simply remarking that he had nothing to do with bills, that he held for his money a bond and sasine over lands yielding a rental that would pay his interest six times over, and he was quite independent of everybody. He was, however, at length persuaded by a friend to send his bond and sasine to a respectable Glasgow law agent of experience, to examine them and see that they were correctly drawn, since from Mr C——'s conduct in other respects even his accuracy was not to be trusted. The agent he employed happened to be Mr Fell, the agent of Mr M——, the discounter of the £200 bill. This was of great importance, seeing that he was already well acquainted with C——'s transactions. After perusing the bond and sasine, what first attracted his notice was the name of the estate and description of the lands. He was pretty well acquainted in the parish in which the lands were said in the description to be situated, yet he never had heard of the lands described, and he thought lands of that extent could hardly be situated in that parish without his having heard of them. To make more certain, however, he wrote to the minister of the parish, with a copy of the description of them, and the name of the proprietor and granter of the bond, requesting to know if there were such lands, and a proprietor of the name stated, in his parish. The lands mentioned in the bond and sasine were "Bailies Hill, Inchfauld, Holmriggs, and Braemyre, with parts, pendicles, and pertinents," &c. &c., and the owner thereof and granter of the bond was "James Freeling." The clergyman returned an immediate answer in the following terms:—

"MANSE OF ——, *3d February* 18—.

"SIR,—I have received your letter of the 1st instant. There are no lands of the names or description mentioned by you situated within this parish, and no proprietor or person whatever of the name of Freeling resident therein; neither are there any such lands or person of that name within any of the adjoining parishes. I have been minister of this parish for upwards of thirty years, and know intimately all the lands and every proprietor in this district of the county, and I can say with perfect safety that there are no lands of the names given, or any proprietor, great or small, of the name of Freeling resident within the district. There must therefore either have occurred some singular mistake, or more probably some gross fraud has been practised. I shall be happy to afford you any further information in my power, and shall be curious to hear the result of your inquiries.—I am," &c.

Mr Fell's worst fears were now realised. It would seem that C—— had not only given his unfortunate employer the names of fictitious lands, and that of an imaginary owner who did not exist, but had actually made out in that owner's name a bond and disposition in security, and had adhibited his name to it as the granter. Yet the thing was so perfectly unprecedented in the annals of conveyancing that for a long time Mr Fell could hardly believe in so extraordinary a fraud, or fully realise its existence. Indeed, on looking at the instrument of sasine, he could not help clinging to the hope that the name of the county of Lanark must be a mistake, and that the lands would be found in another county, for the sasine bore to be duly recorded, and had adhibited to it the certificate of the keeper of the General Register of Sasines in Edinburgh. It was hardly conceivable that any man in his senses would present and cause to be recorded a sasine over fictitious lands, as the trick could not fail to be speedily discovered by one or other of the numerous parties who are constantly engaged searching the general record. To solve the doubt, therefore, Mr Fell went by coach to Edinburgh, carrying with him the bond and sasine, and calling at the General Register proceeded to examine the minute-book. To crown his amazement, he found that the sasine had never been recorded, and on exhibiting it to the substitute-keeper, whose name was adhibited to the certificate of registration endorsed thereon, he pronounced the certificate false and fraudulent, and his signature a gross forgery.

Mr Fell was now fully enlightened, and his astonishment knew no bounds. Affixing one or more fictitious names to a bill was a thing he had often heard of, and was not unfrequent in the history of crime; but here was one of the most complicated pieces of fraud he had ever heard of, or of which he could form any conception. A bond had been made out with a description of fictitious lands, with an imaginary owner, who bore to subscribe it, and with the names of C——'s own clerks forged as the attesting witnesses. Then an instrument of sasine was made out as following on the bond, with the name of C—— himself prostituted as the attesting notary, with the names of two witnesses to the act of infeftment forged, with a fictitious certificate by the keeper of the record, certifying falsely that the instrument was duly registered, and with the keeper's signature thereto also forged. The thing exceeded any act of swindling and forgery hitherto known.

There next devolved on Mr Fell the unpleasant duty of acquainting Mr L—— of the ruinous act of swindling and fraud to which he had been subjected, and of the total loss, so far at least as the pretended security was concerned, of his £2000.

He held out to him, however, the hope of recovering a considerable part of his money by taking measures, the same as the different holders of the forged bills were doing, for attaching and selling C——'s property in Lanarkshire, consisting of a valuable farm. Poor Mr L—— was thunderstruck at the intelligence, but immediately authorised his agent to follow the course recommended. Mr C—— had a law agent in Glasgow who, it would seem, had had a great deal of trouble in assisting him to manage his pecuniary affairs. He had conducted a considerable deal of personal and other law-suits on his behalf, and had besides made large advances of money for his accommodation. He informed the other creditors and Mr Fell, that eighteen months previously, having pushed C—— for a settlement of his claims against him, he had got from him an heritable security over his estate. C—— had previously borrowed a sum of £4000 over it, but this, his agent said, was paid up, and he had received a security over it for £6000. His agent was shewn by C—— a discharge and renunciation of the £4000 debt duly recorded in the Register of Renunciations, upon which the former took a bond for his debt of £6000. He considered the property worth £8000, and he informed the creditors that if it fetched £8000 there would be a surplus of £2000 for division among them after paying his bond of £6000.

In a short time C——'s agent, the holder of the £6000 bond, was waited on by another practitioner, the agent for one of the banking companies, who held a bill for some hundred pounds which the bank had discounted for C——, and he informed him that having considered it his duty to search the register, he found in it the sasine for the £4000 debt, and also that for his £6000 one, but he found no renunciation recorded of the former of these sums. This somewhat alarmed the bond-holder, but as he had the renunciation of the first bond with a certificate endorsed thereon by the keeper of the record, he felt quite secure; nevertheless he went to the register and turned it up at the date of the certificate, but found no renunciation there recorded. He at once went to the keeper of the record, to whom he shewed the renunciation and relative certificate, who at once told him that the certificate was fictitous and the signature to it a gross forgery. He in the last place went to the creditor in the £4000 bond, who, on the renunciation being exhibited to him, pronounced the signature of his name thereto a most decided forgery. It thus appeared that nearly every person concerned in C——'s affairs as creditors were grossly defrauded and serious sufferers. His property in Lanarkshire was soon afterwards brought to sale, and realised only £8000. It thus appears that C——'s own agent lost upwards of £2000; the poor Roxburghshire farmer lost the whole of his £2000; four different banking-houses lost the amount of six discounted bills, amounting in all to £4500—making the whole loss thus amount to £8500. So daring an instance of swindling and forgery had not occurred since the case of Fauntleroy.

It only remains to mention the real fate of C——. He was not drowned as stated on occasion of the wreck of the ship *Enterprise*, but, on the contrary, was safely landed at Bristol along with the portion of the passengers and crew that were rescued. When a gentleman entered a coffee-room at Bristol where a number of the persons rescued were seated, and asked if a passenger named Webster was known to any of them, as noticed above, the person who answered so promptly that he was drowned was no other than Webster (C——) himself. He at once perceived from the inquiry made that his case had become a matter of public notoriety, and he acted accordingly. He instantly made his way to Plymouth and took his passage for the continent. A number of years passed and his name and transactions had almost been forgotten, it having been universally understood that he was drowned on board the *Enterprise*, when one morning a gentleman in Scotland, to whom he had on one occasion done a special service, though he had afterwards cheated him, received the following letter :—

"BRUSSELS, *6th October* 18—.

"DEAR SIR,—You will be surprised to receive this epistle from one whom you doubtless for a long time have thought to be numbered with the dead; and, alas! the realisation of that event is now not far distant. My life since I left Scotland has been an extremely chequered one, and full of vicissitudes and troubles. Instead of being drowned, as was universally believed, I was among those who were saved from the wreck of the *Enterprise*. Having been landed at Bristol along with the other survivors, I immediately discovered that my name had become notorious, and that a warrant had been issued for my apprehension. To divert this catastrophe I caused it to be stated that I had been drowned—a statement which I found entered all the public prints, and to prevent discovery I immediately left Bristol and went to the continent, living at various towns under a feigned name.

"The first place where I made my *debut* on the continent was Paris, the salons and society of which were so attractive that, until admonished by the speedy diminution of my finances, I lived for some time in a state of elysian bliss, oblivious of the past and regardless of the future. At length, to repair my wasted exchequer, I in an evil hour resorted to the gaming-table. The hells of Paris are proverbial. The loads of gold which captivated the eye were sights too exciting to be resisted by a needy and reckless adventurer. *Rouge et noir* was the game.

Staking low at first and being successful, I increased my stakes, and, strange to say, I left the table at a late or rather an early hour one morning a large gainer. Though I entered the house worth less than £50, I retired from it the master of from £4000 to £5000 sterling. Had prudence now come to my aid and made me quit the allurements of gaming, I might have lived in great comfort, but my evil genius as usual had the mastery. I repaired to the same den of vice for a number of evenings, and being always more or less excited with wine, night after night my finances gradually diminished, till, alas! one evening having experienced a continuous run of bad luck, my large means were actually diminished to a hundred francs, and staking the whole of this sum in despair, it was swept from me like the rest, and I was thus wholly ruined and rendered penniless.

"I will not trouble you with all the details of my subsequent career of life. I sought employment as a menial of the humblest description, but my imperfect knowledge of the language was a serious impediment. I managed, however, to procure employment as assistant boots or porter at the most inferior hotels or places of entertainment in different towns. I at length found means of being employed as assistant-waiter in an English hotel kept at Brussels—a situation I managed to retain for some years, till increasing habits of dissipation caused my dismissal. I next descended to become marker in a low billiard-room in one of the meanest localities of this city, being barely able to earn a sum sufficient for my sustenance in the plainest and poorest style. I at length was seized with a fever which prostrated me for some weeks, during which time I was supported in an hospital as a pauper. I recovered from the fever, but only to be the victim of extreme weakness, and with my lungs almost entirely gone. The medical attendants assure me that I cannot survive beyond ten days or a fortnight.

"It is a strange course to appeal to a gentleman whom I once so seriously wronged and injured. Yet looking at the other side of the account, and recollecting that I once rendered you a service, I venture to appeal to your sympathy by requesting the remittance of a small sum to soothe, and in some measure comfort a human being, the tide of whose life is fast ebbing, during the few days that remain to him on earth. I am at this moment a wretched pauper in a foreign land, with hardly a shred of clothing to cover my wasted frame, with the scantiest pittance of coarse food, and sunk to the greatest depth of misery and suffering. I feel unable to write more.—I subjoin my address, and remain, your afflicted friend,

"W—— C——."

The gentleman to whom this letter was addressed, who was perfectly astonished at seeing it, lost no time in writing to a friend in Brussels, enclosing a considerable sum for the relief of the writer. He received an answer giving the most affecting description of the miserable condition in which he found the latter, stretched on a bed of straw among the lowest of the diseased paupers, in an hospital set apart for the poor of the meanest grade. He procured a comfortable lodging for him in the near neighbourhood, with a proper bed, and all the necescaries of life suitable to his case, with a paid medical attendant. He only survived a fortnight, and his remains were decently interred by the same gentleman who had attended to his comforts during the last fortnight of his life. Such was the sad end of the wholesale forger and swindler.*

* The above is substantially a true narrative of a case which occurred twenty or thirty years ago. Several fictitious deeds were made out and passed off as genuine by a person who fled from justice, and the names of parties, witnesses, and keepers of records were forged as above stated, as were a number of bills that were discounted, and the holders defrauded of their amount. But the names of the persons concerned are not given above, nor are the places there mentioned the real *loci delicti*.

INSANE CRIMINALS.

Of late years no part of criminal procedure has caused greater difficulty or created more discussion than that which occurs in determining what amount of mental aberration entitles the accused party to exemption from punishment. The range is so vast between the condition of the furious maniac and the man whose mind apparently exhibits mere eccentricities of fancy, that a correct estimate of a prisoner's state of mind is often the most difficult of medical problems. The case of that class of lunatics termed monomaniacs is often so perplexing as to cause the most annoying puzzle to medical men as well as to judges and juries.

Thus a man who mixes with society and manages important affairs is often found on some one point to be wholly incoherent and with his mind completely distorted, while on every other it is apparently sound and rational. Some instances of these will be noticed.

I. THE IMAGINARY BARON.

Mr J—— B——, a respectable inhabitant of a fishing village in the west of Scotland, carried on a considerable trade in herring-fishing and fish-curing, being part owner of two fishing-smacks, and occupying a store in which he conducted the business of curing herrings. His business was managed systematically and with success, and he was respected by his neighbours. It was known, however, to his nephew and niece, who lived in family with him, and to his more intimate friends, that his mind was affected with the very singular hallucination of imagining that he was a lord, and the owner of an estate and castle in the neighbourhood, both belonging to a nobleman. So long as the nobleman and his family did not come to reside in the castle, B—— was perfectly quiet, but when they did reside, which they frequently did, it was with the utmost difficulty that his friends could restrain him from going to the castle and using violence for their expulsion.

On one occasion Lord —— and his family and servants came to reside in the castle during part of the shooting season. Mr B——'s nephew and niece happened to relax in their usual watchfulness, and his lordship's arrival having come to B——'s knowledge, he forthwith provided himself with a large bludgeon, and, proceeding with all despatch to the castle, he rung the bell with great violence, and, after pouring torrents of abuse on the servant who answered the door, dealt him a severe blow with his bludgeon on the head, which felled him to the floor. The cries of the servant thus assaulted speedily brought other two to his rescue, and B—— being disarmed of his bludgeon, was secured until two police constables were brought, who carried him before a magistrate, by whom, after examination, he was committed for trial. It would appear that the blow inflicted on the servant who opened the door was very severe, and that his head was seriously cut and injured. B—— was accordingly cited for trial before the sheriff of the county with a jury. The libel charged him with an aggravated assault on Alexander Thomas, Lord ——'s servant, to the effusion of blood and serious injury of his person. The sheriff having explained to B—— the nature of the charge against him, and afterwards put the usual question whether he was "guilty or not guilty," the latter, who was in a state of great excitement, said in a loud voice, "I am not guilty. Everybody has a right to protect his own property, and to turn all intruders out of his house. I am proprietor of the estate of —— and —— Castle, and nobody has a right to take possession of them without my leave."

This statement being technically a plea of not guilty, a jury was empannelled to try the case. The servant who was assaulted, and his two fellow-servants who came to the rescue, were examined, and proved the assault. The prison-surgeon and another medical man, both of whom had visited the prisoner several times since his commitment, and were also present in court from the beginning of the trial, were next examined as to the state of the prisoner's mind, and both swore that they considered him to be affected with monomania. They were of opinion that the prisoner, labouring under the extraordinary delusion of believing that the estate and castle referred to were his own, was unconscious of having committed any wrong act, and was insane at the time the act charged was committed. The procurator-fiscal having addressed the jury for the crown, and the solicitor for the prisoner for the defence, the sheriff charged the jury, who returned a verdict finding that the acts charged in the libel were proved, but that the prisoner laboured under insanity at the time he committed them, and was incapable of judging between right and wrong. The sheriff, accordingly, in respect of his insanity when the acts were committed, found him not accountable for them, but ordained him to be imprisoned subject to the future orders of court. The prisoner was subsequently sent on the proper warrant to an asylum for lunatics, where he was permanently confined.

What was peculiar in this case chiefly was, that the accused, with the exception of a few slight peculiarities, was not only perfectly sound on every point except one, but even conducted a considerable business with regularity and success for a number of years.*

II. THE IMAGINARY PRINCE.

Eugene E. A. Whelps was tried before the High Court of Justiciary at Edinburgh in July 1842, for aggravated assault by means of stabbing and with intent to murder, under the statute of George the Fourth. He seems to have been a vagrant, and to have come from England to Dunbar, where, having partaken of some spirits and become disorderly on the streets, he attracted a crowd of boys after him. The keeper of the prison observing the disturbance in the town took Whelps into custody, and while doing so was stabbed by him with a knife. Whelps was thereafter taken before a magistrate, examined on the charge of assault, and finally committed for

* The author was present at the trial above referred to, and the occurrences stated actually took place as mentioned.

trial on the above charge of assault, under the statute applicable to assault by cutting and maiming.

On his examination he stated that he was a native of London—a son of the late Duke of York—and the true heir to the British crown; that he had been removed to Ireland for the purpose of preventing him from succeeding to his uncle George the Fourth. While from this part of his declaration, as well as from other evidence, it plainly appeared that the accused laboured under the delusion that he was heir to the British throne, it on the other hand was evident, from the remaining part of his declaration, that on every other subject he was sound and free from any illusion. Thus when questioned as to the stabbing, he first parried the question and then denied the charge. He admitted having had a knife in his possession at the time he was apprehended, but he said though he may have taken it out to frighten the prison-keeper, he did not stab him or use it against him in any way. In short, he seemed perfectly alive to the criminality of assaulting the keeper, and of the importance to him of preventing the charge from being proved.

The public prosecutor having seen fit under the circumstances to depart from the graver charge under the statute, and he having addressed the jury for the crown, and the prisoner's counsel for the defence, the judge charged the jury. The assault was fully proved, and the only point of difficulty in the case related to the state of the prisoner's mind. His counsel did not insist on the plea of insanity, since it might involve the perpetual confinement of his client. The jury accordingly found the prisoner guilty of the assault, but though they considered him sufficiently aware, at the time of committing the act charged against him, that he was infringing the law, yet being of opinion that his intellect was somewhat weak, recommended him to the lenity of the court. The court sentenced him to six months' imprisonment.

This case differed from that of the fish-curer mentioned in the last section in this material respect,—that in the case of the former, the offence charged arose out of the matter in regard to which the delusion of monomania existed, while in the latter the delusion had no connexion with the act charged.*

III. THE DEVOUT THIEF.

Monomania has not unfrequently been known to assume the character of a propensity to steal, and another remarkable feature of such a phasis of the complaint is, that the propensity is often directed to the theft of some particular article, while no disposition is shewn to appropriate any other.

Upwards of thirty years ago, a great sensation was created in Edinburgh by the Rev. D. M——, the clergyman of a Protestant chapel there, being brought to trial for the crime of theft. The chapel was well attended. The accused was considered exemplary in his walk and conversation, zealous in the discharge of his different duties, and much respected by his hearers. Books had been frequently missed from auction-rooms near the University where weekly sales took place, and where the

* This case is given in the printed reports of the Court of Justiciary.

books were laid out for inspection the forenoon before the sale. For a long time no clue could be found to the theft. There was at that time a reading-room in Hunter Square, with a small room at the entrance-door, in which were usually left by the subscribers their umbrellas, books, or parcels, which they might have. A man of colour was door-keeper, and had charge of the rooms. A gentleman connected with the auction-rooms spoken of, who was a subscriber at the reading-room, one day on coming out of it observed, while passing the small room, the door-keeper, who usually sat there, reading a book with which he seemed highly amused, and was laughing. He asked what book it was which entertained him so much. The door-keeper shewed him an old Bible illustrated with numerous pictures. The one at which he was so much amused was a representation of the devil dragging a sinner into hell. The gentleman on looking at the book, at once recognised it as having been stolen from the auction-rooms some days before. He asked the door-keeper to whom it belonged, and was told that it belonged to a clergyman, one of the subscribers who was then in the rooms, and had left the book along with his umbrella. On going back into the room he at once saw and recognised Mr M——, who from his dress he perceived was the only clergyman in the room. He, however, resolved to proceed with caution, and instead of at once speaking to the reverend subscriber, went home and informed the head of the auction establishment what he had seen. The porter who had charge of the rooms where the books were exhibited being spoken to, said he noticed the Rev. Mr M—— in the rooms examining the books almost every time a sale was to take place. He said he thought he saw him going away once or twice with books under his arm, very like those which were on the tables, but as he often had one or more books under his arm on entering the rooms, and as his profession placed him above suspicion, he was thrown entirely off his guard. The auctioneer finally determined to apply for a warrant to search the reverend gentleman's house, and on obtaining it, he employed an experienced detective with assistants to carry the warrant into effect. Accordingly, in searching the library in Mr M——'s house they found a great number of books which were identified as having been stolen from the auction rooms referred to, at different times, and among others the Illustrated Bible which first led to a detection.

The case now assumed so serious an aspect that it was handed over to the procurator-fiscal of the sheriff court, who got the reverend gentleman apprehended, examined, and finally committed for trial. The accused's judicial declaration was confused and contradictory. He could give no proper account of where he bought some of the numerous books with the theft of which he was charged, or how he came by them, while in regard to others he admitted that he may have taken them from the auction-rooms, but assigned no reason why he took them, or did not return them on finding that he had brought away books not belonging to him, and he repeatedly said that the books were his, and that he had a right to them, and appeared quite indifferent to the charge, expressing great surprise at his being detained, and let slip one or two remarks that he had a right to take books wherever he found them.

It was remarked by the sheriff and procurator-fiscal, as a matter of surprise, that he did not seem to feel the vast importance to his case of accounting for the manner in which the books came into his possession, and seemed to view the circumstance of having the books in his custody as a thing of the most trivial consequence, and even as if he were entitled to take them.

The trial took place before the Justiciary Court. On the indictment being read over charging the accused with the theft of a great variety of books, his counsel entered a plea of not guilty. The auctioneer at the college and other two booksellers proved that the books produced were their property, and that they were found in the prisoner's custody. The crown counsel pointed out to the jury that the prisoner, while admitting that he was in possession of the books mentioned in the indictment, which were proved not to be his own, could give no satisfactory account of the manner in which he became possessed of them. The Illustrated Bible, too, was dwelt on as a damning circumstance, having been found two days after being taken away in custody of the accused, who was carrying it by itself, and who must have known that he had taken it away, and to whom it belonged.

Exculpatory evidence was adduced for the prisoner of a number of men of the highest character and standing. They spoke to his unaffected piety and zeal in the discharge of his duties—his liberal contributions to benevolent and charitable objects—his untiring perseverance in visiting the sick—his perfect disinterestedness and the absence of every selfish feeling in his conduct generally. Yet all this, to the court and jury, and all who did not know him intimately, only served to give a decided impression that he was a most profound hypocrite. The prisoner's counsel touched on the confused state of his client's mind, but was afraid actually to aver insanity, since it might involve his permanent imprisonment, though he was perfectly aware he was a monomaniac. The counsel on either side being heard, and the presiding judge having charged the jury, the latter, in conformity with the judge's charge, returned a unanimous verdict of guilty.

He was sentenced to seven years' transportation beyond seas.

All the prisoner's intimate friends were perfectly aware of his peculiar distortion of mind in regard to books. If he borrowed a book he would never return it until it was called for and delivery demanded, yet in every other transaction he appeared to be straightforward and punctual, and to exhibit no selfish disposition, but quite the reverse. He paid all monies due by him with perfect regularity and promptitude. He was the collector and custodier of numerous sums of money collected for charities and benevolent institutions, all of which he paid most accurately, though he might with ease have appropriated portions of them without detection, and always added liberal contributions of his own fully proportioned to his means. Neither did it appear that he ever sold or disposed of, for money, any of the books which he had taken, though no fewer than four copies of a French dictionary, all of them by the same author and of the same edition, were among the stolen books. His intimate associates were satisfied that a decided hallucination pervaded his mind that it was his peculiar right and his province to appropriate all books wherever he could find them.

IV. THE LIVING MIRROR.

Before the sitting magistrate of the Glasgow Police Court, a respectably-dressed man, named John Langford, was brought up one forenoon, charged with being the cause of collecting crowds on the streets, and obstructing the passengers. It appeared, from the evidence of several constables, that the accused imagined himself to be composed of glass. He moved along the streets with great caution; and in passing from the side pavement to the centre of the street, with a view to cross to the other side, he took hold of each limb alternately with both his hands, raising them with great caution, in case they should be broken. When he observed any person coming in an opposite direction, running or walking fast, he appeared in great trepidation, in case he might be jostled or knocked over and broken in pieces by the fall. These peculiarities, which became known to the public, attracted crowds wherever he was seen, but more especially in the more crowded thoroughfares. But what principally attracted crowds was, that he not only believed his body to be composed wholly of glass, but he imagined that the front of his body was a mirror. The consequence was, that crowds of boys would assemble in front of him for the pretended purpose of adjusting their neckcloths, each affecting to do so while the others were waiting their turn. The poor man would stand with the utmost patience, with his arms expanded, to allow the young rogues to perform their feigned toilets.

Evidence to the above effect having been adduced, and the accused called on for his defence, he said, addressing himself to the sitting magistrate, "My body is composed of glass, and the front of my body is a mirror. If crowds follow me, or make use of me as a mirror, it is no fault of mine. I don't ask them to do so, and I make no disturbance myself." It appeared from the evidence of the witnesses who were examined, that the prisoner was in no respect violent, but, on the contrary, perfectly quiet and inoffensive. The disturbances on the street arose from the peculiar delusions under which he was known to labour having attracted crowds on the streets to obtain a sight of him. In these circumstances, the magistrate directed the officer to deliver him over to some of his friends who attended to witness the result of the case, enjoining them not to allow him to traverse the streets in future.*

V. THE GOVERNESS.

Sir George and Lady L——, who had a mansion in the east of Scotland, resided there during a great part of the year with their daughter, a young lady of eighteen, their only child. Miss B——, a young woman of six or seven and twenty years old, resided also in the family in the capacity of Miss L——'s governess,—a situation which she had filled for a number of years. She was a highly accomplished and intelligent person, with a refined taste and

* This is a real case. The author frequently saw the accused on the streets of Glasgow.

extensive information. She was thoroughly conversant with most of the modern languages; while her attainments in music were of the highest order. Her pupil was a talented young lady, and, as might be supposed, had profited largely by the tuition of Miss B——, who was a most valuable instructress, and a great favourite with the family, and with all who knew her.

Miss B—— had been subject for some time to neuralgia and nervous headaches, and was periodically confined to her room, and often to her bed, by these distressing ailments. Soon after recovering from one of them, she was observed to be somewhat excitable and restless. She could not settle continuously to reading or any other occupation, and her conversation, though not without import, was sometimes incoherent, and her ideas appeared often to have no natural association. Her pupil, on entering the parlour one morning where she and her governess usually read and went through the prescribed tasks of the former, was amazed to see her instructress reclining on two chairs, with her bare head out at a window, which she had opened for the purpose, though it was a cold and damp day in the month of November. She asked the meaning of such a proceeding, and remonstrated with her on her conduct, reminding her of her serious ailments, which such exposure to cold could not fail to increase and aggravate. Miss B—— remarked that a cool head was essential to the health of the body; and that in order to prosecute with success any occupation requiring mental exertion, it was indispensable to have the head perfectly cool. It was only on her pupil threatening to leave the room that she was induced to put down the window. On entering the same parlour one forenoon, about a week afterwards, the pupil found Miss B—— reclining on two chairs, with her feet and legs projected a considerable way out at the window. The morning was cold, and it rained heavily, and her legs, stockings, and other parts of her dress, were saturated with rain. The pupil expressed her utter surprise, and renewed her remonstrances. The governess remarked, with great earnestness, that by making the feet and legs intensely cold for some hours, she meant to try the effect of it on the system, and strongly recommended to her pupil to follow the same course. She said it would send the blood to the brain, quicken thought, and sharpen the intellectual faculties. The pupil said she could not stand such extraordinary conduct any longer; that she must complain to her mother, Lady L——; and proceeded to leave the room. On seeing this, Miss B—— immediately pulled in her limbs, and closed the window, but sat with her feet, limbs, and dress soaked with water, without taking any means for drying them, or shifting her stockings and clothes.

Miss L——, though she did not leave the room at the time, resolved to inform her parents of the extraordinary conduct she had witnessed on the part of her governess. She accordingly mentioned it to her mother, who was greatly surprised, and began to watch narrowly Miss B——'s future conduct. She had been always somewhat peculiar in her manner; but observation shewed that she had become greatly more so of late than formerly. She had no apprehensions, however, of her conduct, which seemed to have no violent tendency, being in any way dangerous either to her pupil or to any of the household. Her intelligence and accomplishments were so superior, and her instructions had proved so valuable to her daughter, that Lady L—— felt the utmost reluctance to remove her from their family. Besides, she thought the recent vagaries of Miss B—— the mere result of some nervous excitement consequent on her late illness, and which were mere eccentricities, that would soon pass away as she convalesced.

Nothing further of any note occurred for several weeks. The governess and pupil slept in the same apartment, in separate beds. On one occasion, some weeks after the occurrences referred to, about two o'clock in the morning, the latter observed Miss B—— rising from bed. She paid little attention at first to the circumstance, as she used occasionally to rise during the night for a glass of water. It was clear moonlight; and after the lapse of a few seconds Miss L—— observed that, instead of pouring out water, she took up a table-knife which lay on the toilet-table, where it had been used by the maid in cutting tape, and with one hand tried its sharpness, as if she meant to cut something. Miss L—— thereupon said, "Miss B——, what are you going to do with the knife?" "Oh," replied she, "I am going in to Sir George and Lady L——'s room to cut Sir George's throat; it will save him a great deal of trouble, as he has had several attacks lately of bronchitis." Miss L—— was perfectly shocked, and had nearly fainted away; but by a great effort summoning resolution, and knowing that the only chance of controlling a lunatic was by affecting to humour them, she got out of bed to the floor, and said to Miss B——, with as obliging an air as she could assume, "Oh, you had better wait for a little, till I go for another knife, and I will assist you. It will take two persons to manage Sir George; and I will go and bring a knife immediately." Miss B——, thinking the proposal very judicious, said, "Very well; I will wait till you come back." The pupil accordingly left the room; but the moment she got outside the door she locked it after her, and, rushing into the adjoining room, she pulled the bell three or four times with the greatest violence. She next ran to the staircase, and called over the bannister for help at the very top of her voice. Sir George and Lady L—— and the whole servants immediately started out of bed, and ran to the place whence they heard the cries. The young lady explained to her father as briefly as she could that Miss B—— had become insane,—was about to go to his room to murder him,—and that she (Miss L——) had got out of the room by stratagem, and locked her in by turning the key in the door after her. Sir George immediately armed himself with a sword, and the male servants each with a poker, and, entering Miss B——'s room with lights, they found her in a state of furious madness, and attempting to force open the door. On seeing Sir George she instantly made a thrust at him with the knife. He parried the thrust successfully, and, striking her smartly with the sword on the hand which held the knife, she lost her hold of it, and it dropped on the floor. It was picked up by one of the servants. Miss B—— appeared in a state of fearful excitement. Her face was flushed, and her eyes glared wildly on Sir George and the servants when they entered her room. In short, she had became a furious maniac. Sir George and the male servants seized hold of her by the arms and hands, which they were obliged to tie behind her back. They also tied her feet. She struggled all the time with her whole strength, and tried several times to bite those who held her. Early in the morning, two medical men were sent for, who reported her to be insane, and, after the usual preliminaries, she was consigned to a lunatic asylum by a warrant of the sheriff.*

* A case similar to this in nearly all its circumstances occurred some years since, but in a different part of the kingdom from that stated above.

THE BIGAMIST.

THE laws of marriage are as various as the different states in which they exist. In some states they are extremely complex, in others much simpler. In the former it is often necessary to enter the parties' names in several registers, and to go through different other forms and ceremonies, the omission of any one of which will render the proceeding nugatory, the parties still remaining in point of law single and unmarried.

Mr Swainford, the son of a wealthy London merchant, became intimately acquainted with Miss F——, who resided in a remote part of Wales with her mother, the widow of a major in the army who had died in India. The intimacy arose when Miss F—— was visiting a family in London, relatives of her father. The gentleman professed the most devoted attachment to the young lady, and having soon won her affections, asked her in marriage, and was accepted. He stated a plausible reason for not being able immediately to marry, but mentioned that arrangements for the purpose would be made in a few months. He proposed that in the meantime they might enjoy the society of each other for a few weeks in some remote locality where they would be unknown, and proposed that she should meet him in Scotland the following week. Love is proverbially blind. After objecting to the proposal and declining it, she at length, blinded by attachment and urged by his entreaties, imprudently consented. Under the pretext to her mother that she was to visit a family in Cheshire, she took her departure for Edinburgh. Having met there by appointment, the lovers lived together in the same lodging for upwards of two months, occupying the same bedroom and bed. The northern metropolis, styled *par excellence* "the Modern Athens," and a "City of Palaces," is noted for its beauty and attractions. Its magnificent public buildings—its undulating hills, constituting not one acropolis but many—and studded with monuments and buildings of rare architectural taste—its extensive prospects of sea, river, and mountain-scenery, all combine to make the visitor imagine he has realised the fanciful descriptions of oriental romance. In such a locality the golden hours of bliss passed with peculiar delight. The past was entirely forgotten by Miss F——, and her present real position never thought of. But,

> "Pleasures are like poppies spread :
> You seize the flower, the bloom is shed."

Her mother had discovered that she was not in Cheshire, and hearing that Mr Swainford had disappeared at the same time, she dreaded what had taken place. For some time she could not discover the retreat of the parties; but having at length done so, she repaired to Edinburgh, accompanied by a male friend, and having called on the couple, she upbraided the male runaway for his perfidy, and lectured her daughter on account of her extreme folly. The result was that Mr Swainford promised faithfully to make immediate arrangements for his marriage with Miss F——, which he assured her would be effected in three weeks.

In the meantime he departed for London, and she returned home to Wales with her mother, to make the necessary preparations on her part. Her *trousseau* was prepared with great despatch, and by the end of three weeks was completed.

After Mr Swainford went to London, he wrote her several letters couched in most affectionate terms. Nothing, however, was said by him in any of them as to fixing the time for the marriage ceremony, though she had alluded to that point in every one of her letters. Three weeks at length passed, but no letter came from him since a week previously. Both mother and daughter then wrote him, urging that the time should be fixed for the marriage, but no answer was received. Mrs F——, after a lapse of ten days, wrote to her husband's relative in London, with whose family her daughter was on a visit when the engagement between her and Swainford took place, entreating him to see the latter, to ascertain the cause of delay in fulfilling his promise, and to urge an immediate arrangement for the marriage. A letter was received by Mrs F—— in a few days from her friend in London, mentioning that, on inquiry at Mr Swainford's father, he was told that his son had gone to the continent about a week before, with the view of making an extended tour, and was not expected to return for at least six months. Mrs F—— and her daughter, and especially the latter, were utterly astonished, and deeply mortified at the intelligence. There could now be no doubt as to the intentions of Swainford, and that by grossly false and hollow professions of attachment, he had heartlessly deceived and seduced the young lady.

Mrs F—— herself and her daughter repaired to London, and, accompanied by her husband's relative already referred to,—the gentleman with whom she had corresponded,—waited upon Mr Swainford's father, and related to him the whole circumstances of his son's conduct. The old gentleman professed entire ignorance of the whole affair. His son, he said, had never alluded to the subject or even mentioned Miss F——'s name to him. He said he could do nothing in the matter till his son's return, and even then, as he was of age, and possessed a considerable deal of property in his own right, independently of him, (the father,) he could not concuss him to marry the young lady, however anxious he might be to do so. He concluded by asking, naturally enough, (and this was the weak point of the lady's case,) how she could reconcile it with propriety to go and live alone with a young man in Scotland. The imprudence of this was frankly admitted, but the urgency of young Mr Swainford, and her devoted attachment to him, were assigned as excuses, and she pointed to the solemn promises contained in his letters.

Matters remained in the same state for nearly twelve months, a month or two before the end of which time Miss F—— had born a son, the result of her imprudent visit to Scotland. She was deeply humbled, and overwhelmed with melancholy,—wholly secluded herself from society, and led the life of an isolated being. Soon after the period referred to, the gentleman who had accompanied

Mrs F—— to Scotland, called one day with a copy of the *Times* newspaper, and pointed out the announcement of the marriage of young Swainford to a lady in the south of England. Things had thus come to a pretty pass. But the friend who brought the *Times* mentioned, that when in Scotland, an experienced professional gentleman to whom he had told confidentially the circumstances attending Miss F——'s residence with young Swainford in Edinburgh, had given him some very important hints on the subject of the marriage laws in Scotland, and had expressed a somewhat decided opinion that from the correspondence and all that had passed between the parties while in Edinburgh, Miss F—— could claim Swainford as her husband. Matters being in such a state that they could not be made worse than appearances then indicated, Mrs F—— authorised her friend to repair to Edinburgh, and on a full statement of the circumstances, to take the opinion of the most eminent counsel on the whole case. He was furnished with all the letters which Swainford had written to Miss F—— from first to last, and with a minute and particular statement of all that had occurred between the parties, both in London and Edinburgh. The result was an opinion by two most eminent counsel of the Scotch bar, that Miss F—— was most decidedly, by the law of Scotland, and by international law, the married wife of Edward Swainford, and that going through the ceremony of marriage with any other woman was nothing more nor less than an act of bigamy on his part. They held that a promise to marry, such as his letters contained, followed by cohabitation, and by his holding out to every person with whom they came in contact that Miss F—— was his wife, clearly constituted a marriage by the law of Scotland.

The opinion obtained in Edinburgh, and the whole information and documents were next laid before Messrs H—— & S——, London solicitors of the highest character and experience, by whom a case for the opinion of eminent English counsel was prepared. and an opinion obtained confirming that of the Scotch lawyers, and recommending an instant prosecution for bigamy. The course recommended was followed without delay. After a correspondence with the intelligent writer to the signet in Edinburgh, who had obtained the Scotch opinion, and by whom a full precognition was taken of all the witnesses who could speak to the transactions of the parties in Scotland, proceedings against Edward Swainford were forthwith commenced, and warrant obtained for his arrestment. He had taken a splendid residence at Sussex Gardens, in the neighbourhood of Hyde Park, where he resided with his newly-married wife.

The constables who called to execute the warrant found him engaged at lunch with his wife and a party of ladies and gentleman. He was much surprised at finding it was a warrant for his arrestment. On learning that the warrant was founded on a charge of bigamy, he treated the matter with the profoundest contempt. The idea that he was ever married to, or could be the husband of, Miss F——, never entered his mind, and he treated it as an attempt to extort money by a fictitious and unfounded charge. It was with no small surprise, therefore, to the gay party by whom he was surrounded, and also to himself, that he was conveyed in custody before a sitting magistrate. The examination was of short duration. The prisoner denied the whole charge, and, by advice of his counsel, declined to answer any questions, reserving his statements for the trial. The prosecutor's counsel explained shortly but distinctly the law of the case, produced the correspondence of the prisoner, and two witnesses to prove the leading facts in regard to the transactions in Edinburgh. He was thereupon finally committed for trial before the Central Criminal Court, but was, however, admitted to bail, though on heavy recognizances.

The trial at length came on, and Edward Swainford was placed at the bar arraigned on a charge of bigamy, by reason of a marriage contracted by him with Miss Eliza B——, Emily F——, his first wife, being still alive. He treated the whole affair as a farce, labouring under the delusion that no marriage could be consummated except in church, at an altar, or by a clergyman. He was, however, extremely indignant and exasperated at the idea of the exposure he must submit to by being placed in such a position.

A jury being sworn, a proof was entered into by the counsel for the prosecutor at great length, having first stated with great distinctness what the marriage laws of Scotland were. He first produced the whole letters of the prisoner addressed to Miss F——, which were filled with promises of marriage, and protestations of constancy. He next produced the landlady in whose lodgings the parties resided in Edinburgh, and her two servants. These proved that the lodgings were expressly taken by the prisoner for himself and his wife—that they lived in the lodgings for upwards of two months, occupying the same bed—that he uniformly styled her Mrs Swainford—that several persons called asking for her under that name, and all packages for her (which were numerous) from shopkeepers and tradesmen, were likewise addressed to her by that name. Several shopkeepers and tradesmen were likewise adduced, who swore that the accused had ordered articles for his wife to be sent to the above lodgings, and wrote her address with his own hand as "Mrs Swainford." Miss F——, the prosecutrix, was next examined. Her youth and beauty, no less than her being the daughter of an officer whose name was well known for valorous acts in several distinguished battle-fields, excited the greatest interest in court. A strong sense of her wrongs appeared to banish her natural modesty and timidity, and she gave her evidence with distinctness and accuracy, detailing all the facts as to her being treated in every respect as the prisoner's wife during the whole time of their residence in Edinburgh. She was next cross-examined by the prisoner's counsel, who asked her if she had never lived with any other gentleman in the same way she had done in Edinburgh with the accused. This gave rise to a volley of hisses from the audience. She replied with much indignation that she had not, and expressed a wish not to be subjected to gross insults. The counsel next asked if she considered it a correct course to live as she did in Edinburgh with the accused. She answered that strictly speaking it might not be correct, "But," said she, "when I did so, I thought I had a man of honour and a gentleman to deal with, instead of an unprincipled knave." The audience gave shouts of applause, which could hardly be suppressed, and the prisoner, quailing under the witness's answer, held down his head and concealed his face. The prisoner's counsel perceiving that nothing favourable to his client's case could be elicited from the witness, and that such a line of examination would only tend to prejudice the jury against the prisoner, put no further questions.

Two eminent Scotch counsel were next examined to prove the law of marriage in Scotland. They were allowed to remain in court during the whole trial, and to hear the evidence of all the other witnesses. They gave it as their unqualified opinion upon oath, that the facts brought out by the testimony of the other witnesses clearly established that a marriage between the prisoner and Miss F—— was fully constituted, and that, in point of fact, they were married persons before leaving Scotland.

There was no evidence adduced on behalf of the prisoner.

The second marriage with Miss B—— was next proved by production of the register, and by two witnesses.

The jury were addressed at great length, in a

clear and able speech, by the prosecutor's counsel, and in another, equally long and ingenious, by the counsel for the prisoner. The judge next charged the jury in a luminous speech, commenting fully on the whole evidence, and applying the law of Scotland, agreeably to the distinct evidence of the Scotch counsel, to all the facts elicited from the witnesses. His charge bore strongly against the prisoner. The jury, after a short absence, returned a verdict finding the prisoner guilty of bigamy, as charged. The announcement was followed by the applause of the audience, which the judge could only suppress with difficulty.

The judge then addressed the prisoner as follows:—"Edward Swainford, it is now my painful duty to award the punishment adapted to the crime of which you have been found guilty by an intelligent jury, with whose verdict I most entirely coincide. I regret to say that your case is one of the most aggravated of the kind it has ever been my lot to try in this court, whether I regard the nature of the offence, or the character of the two unfortunate young females who have been affected by your acts. It was not a sufficient protection to the prosecutrix against your attempts at seduction, that she was young, modest, and of a highly respectable family; neither was it sufficient that she was the daughter of an officer distinguished in the military history of his country. After the most solemn protestations of your attachment, you gained her affections, promised her marriage, and obtained a similar promise from her. Availing yourself of the state of her affections, of which you artfully obtained the possession, and having urged her by every argument you could invent, you at length prevailed on her to accompany you to Scotland, where you resided as man and wife. Thereafter you strove to desert her altogether, and to avoid having any intercourse with her, thinking that you had merely committed a dexterous act of seduction. Luckily for her, however, the laws of the country where you resided together are such, that in the trap which you thought you had so adroitly laid for her, you yourself have been effectually caught, and you and she are to all intents and purposes man and wife. After deserting Emily F——, your chosen and married wife, you next thought prope to pay your addresses to another young woma of respectable connexions, Miss Eliza B——, an after gaining her affections in like manner, an getting her to engage to marry you, you wen through the ceremony of marriage with her, an you and she have lived together, and cohabited a man and wife, for a considerable time. I need no describe the sadly painful predicament into whicl you have brought this unfortunate young woman and what her feelings and those of her friends must be at the disclosure now made of your unprincipled proceedings. The sentence of the court is, that you be imprisoned for two years from this date, and then set at liberty."

The prisoner was now fully awakened from his dream of security. Up to the moment when the verdict was returned he regarded the whole proceedings as a thorough farce. He then began to look surprised; but on hearing sentence pronounced he looked perfectly astounded. The strong language of the judge affected him beyond measure, and on hearing the sentence consigning him for two years as a condemned felon, to be immured in a criminal prison, he became deadly pale, and nearly fainted away.

His conviction was followed by an action of divorce at the instance of his wife, the prosecutrix, who obtained judgment of divorce, and a large annual allowance out of his estate.

THE FATAL DREAM.

EDWARD BLAND and James Mapleson, two young men belonging to Yorkshire,—the one the son of a farmer near Skipton; the other the son of a respectable and extensively-employed tradesman of that town,—were educated at the Skipton Grammar School, and, being under able masters, both received a superior education. They were very much akin in tastes and dispositions, and, being associated from their infancy, their ties of friendship were as close as that of two brothers. They had each read of prairie life in the far west of the American States, and of emigrant life in the backwoods of Upper Canada. As generally happens in such cases, they looked at the fair side of the picture, and hence, captivated by its romance, they became possessed with the most intense desire to cross the Atlantic, and have their lot cast among the wilds of Upper Canada. Extensive forests, buffalo, wild deer, and racoon hunts, bagging wild turkeys, quails, partridges, and the endless variety of game abounding in the trackless woods of that colony, were attractions too great in their estimation to be resisted. Considerable opposition and reluctance were exhibited by the parents of both to the proposed exodus; but it was at length overcome, and their consent obtained.

The two youths, elated with their new project, proceeded to make preparations for their departure. Outfits of clothes, boots, shoes, and all the other appendages of an emigrant, were speedily obtained, and a passage secured in an emigrant ship bound for New York from Liverpool. They were advised to take the route by New York, and thereafter to avail themselves of the commodious and cheap steamers plying on the Hudson River and Erie Canal. By this means they avoided the tedious and dangerous navigation of the St Lawrence, and arrived at their destination in half the time they would have taken by the latter route. They travelled in the intermediate or second cabin on the voyage from Liverpool to New York, and also in the steamers on the Hudson River. The voyage from Liverpool to New York was prosperous and agreeable. There were a number of emigrants on board, and of these seven or eight of the more respectable were intermediate passengers. One of them,—a young man from Cumberland, named John Harling, whose destination was also Upper Canada,—drew very much to Bland and Mapleson. He was obliging in manner, and, having a considerable deal of information in regard to the colony of Canada, the two Yorkshire youths found him useful, and an intimacy between them soon sprang up. Mapleson in particular became extremely intimate with Harling; but Bland, who was much more shrewd and penetrating than his friend Mapleson, did not fancy to the same degree their new fellow-traveller. He thought him too fawning and obsequious, and imagined he had once or twice discovered a little duplicity in some of his transactions. He had not that frank, open, and candid manner which accorded with his notions of an eligible associate. He did not, however, allow this to disturb a certain amount of intimacy. Accordingly, the three young men were close associates.

On reaching Toronto, the three youths repaired together to the Government Land Office, and having examined the plans of the numerous blocks of land, and afterwards taken some days to visit them, Bland and Mapleson at length fixed upon a large block on the banks of the Huron Lake, near the mouth of the Wye River, about fifty miles from Toronto, which they bought as copartners, and named Skipton Valley. A portion of the claim had been already cleared, and had a comfortable house,—a circumstance which added considerably to the price. Harling selected a block adjoining that of his two friends, but which had no house, hut, or place of abode of any kind. He, however, prevailed on them to allow him to reside in their house along with them, bearing, of course, his share of the living. This was a prodigious advantage to him, since it saved him the heavy expense in the meantime of building a residence for himself. The parties began immediately to clear timber and cultivate their claims like other backwoodsmen, and to construct sheds for their cattle.

There were a number of highly respectable settlers in their neighbourhood, some of whom had extensive runs, which they had possessed for a number of years, and which were not only fully cleared, but in a high state of cultivation. These settlers the three new immigrants found extremely useful, inasmuch as they not only gave them all necessary information about the best system of management, but lent them occasionally implements of husbandry and horses. An intimacy, accordingly, sprang up between the latter and former. One of the wealthiest of these old settlers had an only daughter of surpassing beauty; and, for the daughter of a backwoodsman, remarkably accomplished. It was not surprising, therefore, that she should, in a more than usual degree, attract the attention of the three new comers, whose removal to the backwoods had nearly deprived them of all society. The young lady, Eliza Fremont, was the daughter of Mr Edward Fremont, formerly an extensive farmer in the county of Norfolk, who had, five or six years previous to the period of which we are speaking, emigrated with his wife, a son, and daughter, to the Canadian colony. Having brought a considerable capital with him, he speedily cleared several large blocks of land, and had afterwards fenced and got them into a state of thorough order and cultivation. The United States had by that time removed the serious restrictions formerly imposed on Canadian produce, in the shape of import duties; and hence Mr Fremont, the annual produce of whose claims—which consisted of wheat and various grains, flour, cattle, horses, and different other commodities—was extensive and valuable, drew a yearly income of several thousand pounds sterling. He had built a fine mansion, with offices, and had a large walled garden, orchard, shrubbery, and pleasure-grounds. Mr Fremont's known wealth, therefore, and superior intelligence, gave him no small position in the district where he resided.

On the very first visit of the three young emigrants to Finchleyhead, (the residence of Mr Fremont,) the family there soon perceived that the two Yorkshire youths were greatly superior to him of Cumberland, in education, intelligence, and general information. The latter, too, besides a good deal of innate vulgarity, and the want of thorough educational training, had a fawning obsequiousness, beneath which lurked a certain degree of sneaking cunning, which became visible after a short acquaintance. The society of the two Yorkshiremen, therefore, was more acceptable, and they met with much more attention from the Fremonts than Harling did. James Mapleson, in particular, was a special favourite. To a thoroughly useful and excellent education, extensive reading and general information, he added an open, frank, and pleasing manner. He was also conversible and communicative. These qualities were not a little enhanced by a handsome face and elegant figure. Miss Fremont had too much discernment not to appreciate both the mental and personal graces which adorned young Mapleson. It was evident, therefore, at every visit, that of the trio, he was the favoured one. Attached as Bland was to his friend, and being, moreover, a man of principle and honour, he was well satisfied to see a mutual attachment springing up between Eliza Fremont and James Mapleson. Not so, however, was John Harling. He formed an ardent attachment to Miss Fremont himself, and thinking that his smooth fawning manner would infallibly give him the preference in her estimation, he was greatly disappointed and exasperated to find another carry the palm. In order to turn the tide, if possible, in his favour, he tried the expedient of throwing out obscure hints, tending to prejudice his two associates in the estimation of the family at Finchleybead. Besides the bad taste displayed in such insinuations, the family at once perceived its object, and it only served to lower him extremely in their estimation. They knew, moreover, the vast obligations he was under to his two associates, for giving him, at inconvenience to themselves, the share of a comfortable house to live in gratuitously, when he had none of his own. He accordingly became morose and dejected, and made himself absolutely disagreeable to the two friends from whom he had received so much kindness. Mapleson thought that his dejection and disagreeable manner were caused by a slight attack of ague, which he had had some days previously; but Bland, as usual, much more discerning, had no difficulty in tracing the true source of their new associate's conduct. He thought, however, that, as happens in similar cases, it would soon abate, and finally pass away. Though he did not like Harling, and had no high opinion of him, yet he thought in the main he was not void of principle.

Mapleson's visits to Finchleyhead were frequent, and acceptable to the family. His attentions to Miss Fremont were marked and unremitting, and at each successive visit were becoming more and more acceptable to the young lady. One clear, calm summer evening, he and she had a long walk on the banks of the Huron Lake. They reached a beautiful promontory, from which this magnificent prince of lakes was visible as far as the eye could carry. Its lovely blue surface lay at their feet, and its numerous wooded islands, as varied in size as in form, feasted the eyes of the beholders. The *tout ensemble* presented a picture of beauty and grandeur baffling all powers of description. It was while the happy couple were seated on a rock, wrapped up in admiration of the fairy scene before them, that Mr Mapleson ventured to put the delicate question, the answer to which was to make him happy or miserable. The lady's cheeks were immediately suffused with crimson. She looked to the ground, and remained speechless. At length he said, "I presume I am to conclude that silence implies consent." She still remained mute, but placed her hand in his. He then took her to his arms, pressed her to his bosom, and imprinted several kisses on her crimsoned cheek. In a few minutes, her emotion subsiding, she recovered her speech, and grasping his hand in both hers, she said, "O James, I am completely happy." The myrtle-bough was thus fairly twined, an unmistakable compact formed, and two lovers made as happy as the perfect consummation of the wishes of both at this stage of their career could make them. The parties walked home slowly, but with the most pleasing feelings in each other's society. It was the setting sun only that admonished them how provokingly swift time seemed to fly. At length, on arriving at a turn of the road near Finchleyhead, they met Mr Harling, who, instead of stopping as they did to speak, brushed past with a slight inclination of the head, and with an extremely sullen air. They ascertained that he had called at Finchleyhead, and seemed much disappointed on learning that Miss Fremont had gone to walk with Mr Mapleson. The cause of his manner and conduct, therefore, on meeting the latter and Miss Fremont, it was now impossible to mistake. After conducting Miss Fremont to her father's residence, and promising, at her urgent request, to call for her on the second evening thereafter, Mapleson returned home to his own station.

In a claim like that of Bland and Mapleson, where a portion .of cleared land bearing crops adjoins a wooded or uncleared portion, game of every kind is always abundant, as the woods afford them a secure retreat, and the crops growing on the cleared portion an ample supply of food so conveniently placed. Hence trespassers or poachers in quest of game from the surrounding country were constantly found on Bland and Mapleson's lands. Though, in a country where game is so abundant, poaching is not treated as a grave offence, or dealt with as in the mother country, yet land-owners are entitled, unless where they permit or encourage the destruction of game, which they sometimes do, to protect their lands and the game thereon, and to prosecute the trespassers. The above two immigrants accordingly, who wished not only to supply their own tables, but could turn the game to profitable account, placed notices at the boundaries of their lands prohibiting all trespassing under the threat of a prosecution. Notwithstanding this precaution, they received private information that several lumberers from the neighbouring rivers, and labourers from the adjoining estates, were in the frequent habit of coming with guns at night, particularly in moon-light, and killing large quantities of game. It was accordingly resolved by Bland and Mapleson to watch the places where poaching occurred, and to get the poachers prosecuted and fined. They therefore fixed the following evening to watch the intruders. They directed two of their servants acquainted with the inhabitants of the neighbourhood to accompany them. Harling had become sullen and disagreeable in his manner, and extremely disobliging, particularly to Mapleson; and his usual power of concealing his sentiments and assuming a courteous manner, had apparently forsaken him. Nevertheless it was judged proper by the other two gentlemen to invite him to join the party. Although the watching was not to take place on his block, and although his lands were differently circumstanced from theirs, only a small portion of his being cleared, yet he had at least some interest to put down poaching. He, however, declined the invitation, on the ground that he had occasion to go to the smithy and to see some labourers whom he appointed to meet with. Accordingly, a few minutes before they went to watch, they saw him go away in the direction of the smithy.

Bland and Mapleson, accompanied by their two servants referred to, set out for the spot where they had arranged, after mature consideration and discussion, to go for the purpose of watching the trespassers. The mode of proceeding was arranged, and the spot where they were to remain concealed was fixed upon, the night preceding, in presence of Harling, who approved of their plans. It was arranged that they should conceal themselves in a small dense clump of maple trees close to the edge of the cleared land. The two Yorkshire gentlemen and their two servants accordingly took their departure as already mentioned, soon after Harling. They were all armed with fowling-pieces, and the two gentlemen had, besides, each a revolver. Not that they intended any violence to the poachers, but simply for self-defence. Besides, almost all persons going abroad in Canada, and particularly at night, or entering woods, are generally armed, to protect themselves from wild beasts. They entered the wood as quietly as possible, and got into the maple clump as had been arranged. The moon was full, and shone brilliantly from a cloudless sky.

After remaining concealed for about an hour in the clump, they heard a rustling noise among the fallen leaves, and footsteps as of a number of persons in the wood, a little to the left of the spot where they stood. In a short time, five men, each with a fowling-piece, emerged from the wood, and came out upon the cleared land, with the view, doubtless, of finding game, of which there was a great quantity on different fields close at hand. They seemed to be in the garb of labourers. The two servants were desired immediately to go forward and endeavour to identify them. They advanced accordingly, and the poachers were somewhat startled, but did not attempt to run away. The servants knew the whole party, and said they were reputed steady respectable men. Two of them were labourers from a property in the neighbourhood, and the other three were lumberers on the river Wye. They expressed their regret at having trespassed—said they had not observed the notices placed on the lands—and did not know the game was preserved. Bland and Mapleson next emerged from their place of concealment, to ascertain what the poachers were saying to their servants. After they left the clump and got a little way on the cleared land, the report of a shot was heard, and some smoke seen issuing from a thicket about a hundred yards to their right, and immediately

Mapleson fell to the ground. Bland instantly saw what had happened, and called out at the top of his voice, "You blackguard, you have shot a gentleman." The five poachers, on seeing what happened, ran forward along with the two servants to assist Mr Bland in raising his friend. He was found, however, to be in a dying state. The poachers assured Mr Bland that the person who fired the shot did not belong to their party. They were five in number only, and were all present, and they knew of no other. Leaving one of the servants along with the poachers to attend to poor Mapleson, Bland and the other servant took up their fowling-pieces and ran off in pursuit of the assassin, in the direction from which the shot came. They heard his footsteps running away, but owing to the time spent in attending to Mr Mapleson, he had got off to some distance. They ran with all their speed, and seemed for a time to be gaining upon him, but after a time he seemed to be gaining ground upon them. Therefore, after a run of some miles through dense wood, they gave up the pursuit, and returned to the dying man. About the same time that the pursuit was commenced, one of the poachers volunteered his services to run for a surgeon of considerable skill, whom he had seen attending a female patient at a house two miles off. The surgeon was found, and arrived at the spot where Mapleson lay, a few minutes after the return of Bland and the servant.

On examining the wound the surgeon pronounced it to be mortal. It was produced by a rifle-ball, which had entered the right side, passed through a portion of the liver, and had entered the regions of the heart. There was an extensive internal hæmorrhage which could not fail to terminate fatally. The poor man had fainted several times—was becoming weaker and weaker, and by the time his friend Bland returned the tide of life was fast ebbing. He was reduced to a state of great weakness, but was quite sensible. At length, fastening his eyes on Bland, and stretching out his hand, which his friend seized hold of, he said, "I am fast dying, nothing can save me. My dear Bland, this is a sad finale to my emigration schemes. Do see Eliza Fremont. Tell her my last thoughts were of her, and that my ardent and devoted attachment continued unabated to the last. Give her my diamond ring and watch. Accept yourself my fowling-piece, rifle, and revolver, and all my books. Send all my other trinkets and valuables to my mother." He then desired Bland to kiss him, and said, "Farewell, my dearest and best friend, God bless and protect you. I hope we will meet in another and better world. I heartily forgive the assassin, whoever he is." Bland's feelings so overpowered him that he cried and sobbed like a child, and could not for some time speak. At length recovering his power of utterance, he said, "My dearest Mapleson, I can hardly stand this scene. I would give everything I am possessed of to restore you, but the Disposer of all human events has ordered it otherwise. I will faithfully obey all your instructions." Bland again embraced and kissed him. He immediately became insensible, and in about half an hour breathed his last. As soon as poor Bland could fully realise the events of the last few hours, he became deeply melancholy, and seemed regardless of everything passing around him. His best and most amiable friend and companion lay stretched beside him a piece of inanimate clay, and he felt himself a solitary and friendless being in the wilds of Canada.

Some of the poachers, all of whom really conducted themselves with great propriety, had run off to alarm the police and constables in the neighbourhood, several of whom had started in quest of the murderer. Bland and the servant who had accompanied him in pursuing and attempting to overtake the person who fired the fatal shot, discovered from the sound of the footsteps that one person only was engaged in the diabolical act. It seemed also quite clear that the shot could not have hit Mr Mapleson accidentally. It was fired from a spot close to the edge of the cleared land, and had hit a person who was on the cleared land, a good many yards from the edge of the wood. There were not at or near the spot any wild quadrupeds, at which alone a rifle would be fired by any person using it for a legitimate purpose. There might be winged game, but a fowling-piece with common small pellets only would be employed against them.

Indeed, it was plain to demonstration that wilful murder was intended; for the shot was no sooner fired than the person who did so immediately ran off with all his might. His footsteps were heard running, and the branches of the trees moving, as he quickly pushed his way through them. Yet there was a strange mystery, and it for a time remained unsolved. Suppose the assassin to be a poacher, there was far too much game in Canada unprotected and easily to be had, to make it worth a poacher's while to shoot at a proprietor for preventing poaching. Besides, Bland and Mapleson had never before watched or interrupted poaching; and so no poacher could come prepared with a rifle to shoot any of them. They were also as plainly dressed on the occasion as their servants, and no stranger could distinguish which was the master and which the servant, or indeed whether they might not be poachers as well as he. The five poachers expressed their firm belief that the person who fired the shot was not a poacher, but some private enemy who knew of Mr Mapleson being to be there, and came purposely to shoot him. They said that a great number of the land-owners encouraged the destruction of game on account of their crops, and every one who chose could get shooting without any difficulty, and it was a thing quite unknown for trespassers to attack land-owners. The body of the murdered man was removed in a waggon to his own and Mr Bland's residence, to await the inquest by the coroner and jury.

The report of poor Mapleson's death spread rapidly in all directions, and made a deep sensation in the neighbourhood, where he was known to everybody, and universally respected. It was also known that he was about to become connected to Mr Fremont's family, which made him a still greater object of interest. Crowds repaired to the spot where the event occurred, to see how it took place. Mr Fremont, on hearing the report, rode over to the deceased's house to ascertain if it was true, and to learn the particulars. He discovered it to be too true, and found poor Mapleson's remains stretched on a table waiting the inquest. He resolved at first to conceal the event from his daughter; but perceiving, on reflection, that it could not be long concealed, and that she must hear of it sooner or later, his next resolution was to break it to her by degrees. But on reaching home, he found that the sad intelligence had already been communicated. His daughter, observing that some important news had reached the servants, who were all talking together, made special inquiry at one of them, who told her that it was reported that something had happened to one of the gentlemen at Skipton Valley, though she did not know to which of them, or at least said she did not. Miss Fremont, of course, became alarmed, and immediately afterwards observing from the window a number of the servants collected round a labourer belonging to an estate in the neighbourhood, who happened to be one of the five poachers above referred to, she ran out, and inquiring at him what had happened at Skipton Valley, was informed by an eye-witness of the catastrophe which had befallen her lover. She instantly fainted away, was carried by the servants into the house, and, after a succession of similar fits, was conveyed to bed, where her father found her on his return home. The shock to her feelings resulted in a fever, which lasted upwards of six weeks. Her health did not fully recover the stroke for more than a year afterwards.

It has been already mentioned that the remains of the unfortunate Mapleson were removed to his own and Mr Bland's house at Skipton Valley to await the inquest. The remains were placed in a room where James Elman, one of the two servants who witnessed Mr Mapleson's death, and the same who, along with Mr Bland, had pursued the assassin, usually slept. There was a large room in which three beds stood, which were occupied by Bland, Mapleson, and Harling. The dead body being placed in James Elman's room, and the door locked, it was arranged that Elman should sleep for a time in the large room, occupying the bed of his deceased master. Harling returned in the course of the evening. He said he had occasion to go to a place, which he named, at a considerable distance, and seemed much fatigued. He mentioned that he had heard at the smithy and several other places on his way, of the sad fate of poor Mapleson, and expressed his deep regret and sympathy for all his friends. He asked to see the body, which he examined, and seemed much affected. He then commented on the imprudence of watching poachers in these remote woods, and being exposed to the attacks of any reckless characters, who might shoot them unperceived and with impunity. After taking supper, they repaired to bed, the two gentlemen and the servant Elman occupying the large bedroom, as had been arranged. The minds both of Mr Bland and the servant were much excited by the events of the evening, and for some hours sleep forsook them. Harling for a short time was also somewhat restless; but in less than an hour he fell fast asleep. He, however, became very disturbed, and evidently had some very troublesome dream. He kept tossing his legs and arms, and muttering something which Bland could not make out. At length, speaking louder and more distinctly, he said, "Oh, I've shot him—I've shot him! poor Mapleson! I wish I had not done it. Oh, I'm sorry I did it. O Eliza Fremont, it was for you I did it; I wish he had got you!" Bland, on hearing this remarkable soliloquy, slipped out of bed, and, moving quietly to the side of the servant's bed, asked him in a whisper if he heard what Harling had said. He replied that he had heard every word of it. His master told him to be sure to remember it, and to listen to any other statements he might make. Bland returned quietly to his bed. He had no sooner lain down than Harling again commenced talking. "Oh, my rifle, my rifle!" said he; "what if they search the large holly tree, and find my rifle; they will at once know it is mine, and find me out. Oh, poor Mapleson! I am a sinful wretch." A number of similar revelations were made by the sleeping man in the course of the night, and all very much to the same effect. Both Bland and his servant became thoroughly convinced that the murderer of poor Mapleson was no other than John Harling. Bland again whispered to his servant to be sure not to say a syllable to Harling himself, or any other person, of what he had heard, till called upon by a magistrate or in a court of law. Soon afterwards they both fell asleep.

Next morning, after a consultation with the servant with reference to the rifle, Bland determined if possible to ascertain for certain whether the rifle was hid, as the dreamer had stated in his sleep. He and the servants had seen Harling on the early part of the previous evening with his rifle in his hand on leaving the house; but two of the other servants, who saw him return late at night, said he then had no gun of any kind in his possession. Bland therefore resolved, first by inquiries in an indirect way, to see what Harling would say about his rifle. He told the servant to clean his own rifle and revolver after breakfast. On Harling entering the breakfast-parlour in the morning, Bland said to him, "I have just been giving orders to the servant to clean my rifle and revolver, as there is no saying how soon we may be attacked, even in the house, by some ruffian. Give yours to him also." And the servant being in the room at the time, he said to him, "Go and get Mr Harling's rifle and revolver, and clean them along with mine." Harling replied, in a somewhat confused manner, "Oh, in coming home last night I had some things carrying, and, being tired, I left my rifle at Miller's house at Grandford" (naming the house of a settler three miles distant) "with one of the servants." Bland lost not a moment in seeing the servant who was cleaning the rifle, being the same who slept in the gentlemen's bedroom the night before, and heard Harling talking in his sleep. He told him he intended to ride to Mr Miller's house, where Harling said he had left his rifle, to ascertain if it really was there; that, after doing so, he meant to ride with all despatch to the place where the murder occurred. He directed the servant to walk thither immediately, and wait his (Bland's) arrival. Bland, taking his horse, rode with the utmost speed to Grandford. It was the breakfast hour, and all the servants on the claim, as well as Mr Miller himself, were at home. Bland said his object in calling so early was to ask for a rifle which Mr Harling had left there with one of the servants the night before. Mr Miller said he had not himself seen Mr Harling, and had not heard of his being there, but that all the servants were in the house assembled at breakfast, and he would go and ask them. He did so, and, returning immediately, said there must be some mistake, as none of them had seen Mr Harling since the week before, and no rifle or gun of any kind was left by him at the house. Mr Bland, who deemed it prudent for the present to conceal his object in making the inquiry, remarked that it was of no consequence; that Mr Harling had left his rifle somewhere, and he thought it was there; that they were collecting all their arms, so as to protect themselves, as there was no saying how many assassins there might be lurking about the woods at night. He, however, went away persuaded in his own mind that he had obtained an important link in a chain of evidence. He now galloped with the utmost speed to the place where his friend was shot, and found that his servant, James Elman, had arrived a few minutes before him. After informing Elman that Mr Miller told him Harling had not left any gun at Grandford, and had not been there at all, he asked him if he recollected, the night before, of seeing a large holly tree when they were pursuing the person who shot Mr Mapleson. Elman replied, that he did observe such a tree, and could find it with perfect ease. He said, when he heard Mr Harling, the night before, mention in his sleep that his rifle was concealed there, he at once remembered passing such a tree in pursuing the assassin. He further said, he remembered that it was just about the time the person pursued passed this tree that he began to run with greater speed; and doubtless this arose from his being, at that very spot, disencumbered of his rifle. Poor Bland was so confused and stunned at the time his friend was shot, that he paid no attention to the trees or their appearance, being intent only on overtaking the murderer. He therefore received with great avidity the information of his servant that he could so easily find the large holly tree. Directing the servant to point the way, they walked as quickly as possible, and, after proceeding about a mile from the spot where the shot was fired, they came to a large holly tree. They searched round it, and, among some loose leaves, they observed the but-end of a gun projecting, on taking up which they at once recognised it as the rifle of Harling, and took possession of it.

A thought next struck Mr Bland that they might find traces of his footsteps; but the holly-tree had such a quantity of leaves blown round it, that no footprints were discernible. On going, however, to the thicket from which the shot was fired, they were more successful. It was free of all leaves, and in several places there were spots of bare clay soil without any vegetation. They found, on several of these spots, distinct impressions of feet wearing coarse, heavy shooting-shoes or boots, with large hob-nails. Most of the impressions were confused by one set of steps effacing the others, from frequent walking or treading over them. But they found two places where the impressions were not effaced, and where the person whose feet had made them must have stood still for a considerable time without moving. They were most distinct; and Elman, on seeing them, immediately pronounced the impressions to have been made by Mr Harling's boots, which he knew by being in the constant habit of cleaning them. He said the boots Mr Harling had on the night before were at home, as he put on a drier pair in the morning on going out to attend his labourers. Mr Bland gave Elman his horse, and directed him to ride home as fast as possible, before Harling would return to dinner, and bring the boots to the spot, and to bring another of the servants with him. He at the same time despatched a labourer whom he had employed cutting timber close at hand, for a plasterer whom he was in the habit of employing, and with instructions to tell him to come to him with all despatch on urgent business, and to bring with him two or three pounds of fine stucco. The two servants with the boots were on the spot in half an hour, and the plasterer arrived soon afterwards. On placing the soles of the boots on the impressions in the clay, they were found to fit exactly. Indeed, besides the precise fit of the boots with the impressions, there were important peculiarities in the soles which rendered the identification otherwise complete. In addition to the row of nails, with large square heads, round the edge of the soles and heels of both boots, there was a star formed of similar nails in the centre of each sole, and a cross in the centre of the heel. These stars and crosses were distinctly impressed on the clay, and, when tried, the nails in the boots fitted into them with perfect precision. Nearly half a dozen of witnesses saw this investigation. The plasterer then took a stucco impression from the clay, which agreed mathematically with the soles and heels of the boots.

Mr Bland had thus, with the aid of his servants and others, obtained a chain of circumstantial evidence as conclusive as can well be imagined. He therefore determined that Harling should not sleep another night under his roof, and, sending for two constables, got him forthwith carried before two justices, in a village then called Fowlerbank, about four miles distant. Mr Bland, the two servants, and the plasterer repaired at the same time to the court, where they were examined as witnesses. An able solicitor was sent for, who conducted the prosecution. Harling had also a solicitor as his legal adviser. The court-room was densely crowded by all the gentlemen and respectable persons in the neighbourhood, including among others Mr Fremont and his son. Mr Bland was first examined, and on mentioning the soliloquy pronounced by Harling during sleep, in which he disclosed the fact of his having committed the murder, and revealed the place where his rifle was hid, Harling seemed nearly petrified with fear and amazement. When his rifle was produced, and his boots, and the stucco impressions from the clay, his courage wholly deserted him, and, except for the interference of his solicitor, he would have confessed his guilt. Intelligence of the singular nature of the evidence soon spread from the court-room to the neighbourhood, and a large crowd besieged the doors, who could not gain admission. The two servants and the plasterer were next examined, and confirmed the evidence of Bland in every particular. One of the servants swore to his having heard the soliloquy of the accused during sleep—his hearing him falsely state next morning that he had left the rifle at Mr Miller's—his being present at finding the rifle at the holly-tree, and discovering the footprints. Both servants identified the boots, and the plasterer swore to the impressions on the stucco being faithfully taken from the foot-prints. The accused was then fully committed for trial to the jail of Toronto.

Next day the inquest of the coroner and jury took place at Skipton Valley. A crowd was assembled, but not so large as that at the court-room the day before, a great many being averse to intrude on the premises of a private individual. The same evidence was adduced as that of the day before; in addition to which was that of two medical men who made a *post mortem* examination and had extracted the ball from the wound. An important piece of evidence was brought out in connexion with the ball. It appeared that it was a conical shaped ball, used only in a minie rifle. This species of rifle was at that time extremely scarce in the district where the murder was committed, and indeed throughout the whole colony, having been only recently introduced in the mother country. Excepting the rifles of Bland, Mapleson, and Harling, it was proved that there was only one other minie rifle within thirty miles of Skipton Valley. On trying the ball which was produced, it fitted precisely Harling's rifle. This was another most important piece of evidence, had that already adduced not been amply sufficient. The jury had no difficulty in returning a verdict of wilful murder against John Harling.

The trial came on at Toronto some weeks afterwards. The circumstances having all transpired through the local newspapers, great interest was excited, and there was intense anxiety to gain admission to the court-room, which was speedily filled to overflowing. Harling, on being brought to the bar, was pale and emaciated, and had a haggard and dejected look. He had retained an able counsel to conduct his defence. The same chain of remarkable and powerful circumstantial evidence as had been laid before the justices at the time of his committal, and before the coroner and jury, was again adduced on the part of the prosecution. Every exertion was made by cross-examination to shake the evidence of the witnesses, but to no purpose. As often happens in such cases, it made the evidence more decisive, and the facts more clear and explicit. After able speeches from the counsel on both sides, and a full, clear, and impartial charge from the presiding judge, the jury, after a short consultation, returned a unanimous verdict of guilty against the prisoner.

Justice M——, the eminent colonial judge who presided at the trial, assuming the black cap, addressed the prisoner as follows:—"John Harling, I question if it has ever fallen to the lot of any judge in this colony to try an offender for a crime of a nature so deeply aggravated in all its circumstances as the one of which you now stand convicted by an intelligent and respectable jury. In most cases of murder there are circumstances more or less palliating. It is sometimes the result of temporary passion—of great provocation—of momentary temptation, or the like; but in your case no such motive is to be found. The mode of effecting your diabolical purpose was planned after full time for reflection, and after mature deliberation. Your victim was a most amiable and respectable man, who had treated you with much kindness, who never gave you the slightest cause of provocation, but to whom, on the contrary, you were under very great obligations. It has appeared, in the course of these proceedings, that you had formed an attachment to a respectable young lady in this district, to whom you became a suitor, but who did not encourage your advances; and that it was known to you that this young lady was about to become the wife of the unfortunate young man whom you so barbarously and brutally murdered. Whether, therefore, you acted from invidious pique or vindictive motives—whether you formed the desperate, selfish, but hopeless scheme of obtaining this young lady's hand after murdering the betrothed object of her affections—or whether all these motives were combined, are circumstances best known to yourself. Not the least striking feature of these proceedings is the providential manner in which you yourself were made to reveal, during sleep, a number of circumstances that were the means of leading to full and complete evidence of your guilt. Be specially careful to improve the short time you will have in this world to make your peace with your Maker, by repenting of your transgressions, and seeking pardon through the merits of your Redeemer; for rest assured, that no hope need be entertained by you that your life will be spared. My only doubt is, whether, from the awfully abandoned profligacy, brutal and barbarous conduct, exhibited in your case, I ought not, in pronouncing judgment, to order your body to be hung in chains, as a solemn warning to parties, who, like you, are lost to every feeling of humanity—in whose bosom a sense of gratitude, for even the most signal favours, has no place, and who can coolly practice the most ruthless atrocities. In the meantime, the sentence of the court is, that you be taken from this bar back to prison, detained there to the 3d day of June next, and that on that day you be taken to the common place of execution, and there hanged by the neck till you be dead, reserving to give any future instructions that may be found expedient for the disposal of your body—and may God have mercy on your soul!"

The execution took place on the day appointed, but no order was given as to hanging the body in chains. Harling died penitent, and made a full confession of his guilt.

It was some months after the death of James Mapleson before poor Miss Fremont ventured out of doors, or was seen in public. The sacred promise of Edward Bland to his dying friend was mentioned to Mr Fremont, but he thought it prudent that for a time the message of her departed lover should not be communicated to her, or the memorials of his constancy and attachment placed in her hands. She was still depressed in spirits, and her wonted robust health not fully re-established. Time, however, and a good constitution restored her, and her father at length admitted Mr Bland to the requested interview. Notwithstanding that the young lady was affected with deep melancholy, she received the dying message as to her lamented lover's attachment and constancy quietly, and with a pleasing though sad satisfaction. When the diamond ring and watch were placed in her hands she shed tears, and pressed them to her lips. She thanked Mr Bland most cordially for his great kindness, and for the trouble he had taken on behalf of his departed companion. She said she would ever entertain for him the highest respect and friendship, knowing him to be the dearest and most attached friend and companion of James Mapleson.

Several years passed, Mr Bland was on the most intimate footing with the family at Finchleyhead, and a frequent visitor. Miss Fremont's friendship for him on account of her departed lover continued unabated. His attachment to Miss Fremont, which soon commenced, gradually increased, at length became marked, and his attentions were assiduous. His attainments and worth made him universally esteemed, and he was both handsome and of polished manners. Miss Fremont's friendship ripened into a more tender affection, and both at length became devotedly attached to each other. It is not remarkable, therefore, that Eliza Fremont soon became Mrs Bland, and Mr and Mrs Bland were the most valued acquisitions to the society of the district in which they resided, and occupied a high position.

CPSIA information can be obtained
at www.ICGtesting.com
Printed in the USA
LVHW101934050422
715402LV00003B/51

9 783752 589474